BEAST RIDER

TONY JOHNSTON
and
MARÍA ELENA FONTANOT DE RHOADS

A BOY'S JOURNEY BEYOND THE BORDER

BEAST RIDER

AMULET BOOKS, NEW YORK

Cataloging-in-Publication Data has been applied for and may be obtained from the Library of Congress

ISBN 978-1-4197-3363-5

Text copyright © 2019 The Johnston Family Trust and María Elena Fontanot de Rhoads
Cover illustration copyright © 2019 Edel Rodriguez
Book design by Hana Anouk Nakamura

Quote, top of page 7: copyright © 2002 Sonia Nazario/*Los Angeles Times*

Poem, bottom of page 7: copyright © 1974 Nancy C. Wood, reprinted from *Many Winters*, courtesy of the Nancy Wood Literary Trust (NancyWood.com)

Published in 2019 by Amulet Books, an imprint of ABRAMS.

Printed and bound in U.S.A.
10 9 8 7 6 5 4 3 2 1

Amulet Books are available at special discounts when purchased in quantity for premiums and promotions as well as fundraising or educational use. Special editions can also be created to specification. For details, contact specialsales@abramsbooks.com or the address below.

Amulet Books® is a registered trademark of Harry N. Abrams, Inc.

ABRAMS The Art of Books
195 Broadway, New York, NY 10007
abramsbooks.com

For all Beast Riders
And their broken families

And

For Taketora "James" Tanaka, of the U.S. 442nd
Infantry, the Purple Heart Battalion

—TJ

For our brave and loving countrymen and -women
who smile at life in good and bad times

—MER

SE LO COMIÓ EL TREN.
THE TRAIN ATE HIM.

—Sonia Nazario "Enrique's Journey, Chapter Three, Defeated Seven Times, a Boy Again Faces 'the Beast,' " Oct. 2, 2002.

***

HOLD ON TO WHAT IS GOOD

HOLD ON TO WHAT IS GOOD
EVEN IF IT IS
A HANDFUL OF EARTH.
HOLD ON TO WHAT YOU BELIEVE
EVEN IF IT IS
A TREE WHICH STANDS BY ITSELF.
HOLD ON TO WHAT YOU MUST DO
EVEN IF IT IS
A LONG WAY FROM HERE.
HOLD ON TO LIFE EVEN WHEN
IT IS EASIER LETTING GO.
HOLD ON TO MY HAND EVEN WHEN
I HAVE GONE AWAY FROM YOU.

—by Nancy Wood, from *Many Winters*, 1974.

THE JOURNEY

They say in this place where we live that someday La Bestia, The Beast, will get you. One day if you stray too far, as some of our niños have done, it will grab you and drag you away forever. For a long time I did not believe this, till it took Toño, my brother. In dreams I feel its hot breath on my neck. I hear its fearful scream. I know that sometime very soon I will follow the terrible, tempting voice and The Beast will take me away—or kill me.

C all me Manuel. It is a good name, says Abue, short for abuelita. Mine is a good name my grandmother has told me for as long as I can remember, a good name as good as the land itself. Then slowly, like the priest who sometimes visits this place, she moves one dry brown arm in a widening gesture to point out the dry brown landscape before us. The milpita, little corn plot, which is our life.

Here there are many milpitas, flat flat. Ours and those of our neighbors, all touching each other like the patches Abue sews onto our worn-out clothes.

Our corn plot. Really it is not the dirt itself that keeps us going, but the maíz, the corn, along with pumpkins and frijoles, which spurts up from it. So we tend it with great care. "We are People of Corn," Papi says. "Since time before time our family has tilled this field," he tells me proudly and many times over. "And this field repays us." He pats a small plant with tenderness, saying, "This little green one, one day she will feed us." I know it is true.

The seasons come. The seasons go. Twelve years since I was born. Papi and I and my little brother Javier and little sister Belén turn the earth. We plant the kernels. We tend the plants. Each year, with sun, with rain, with prayers they grow tall tall. I think, when the wind shuffles them, they are shambling and beautiful as old people. And each year they give us corn. But in times of little rain not enough. Then we work harder. We eat less.

We have one ox. We do not name him. Because if he has a name we will mourn him like family when he dies. And it will hurt deep in our hearts. More than being nameless. Even so, deep in my heart I call him Trini.

We have a dog also. Tough and full of life. He *does* have a name, I do not know why, for surely our hearts will feel stabs of sadness when he goes. Anyway, he is Guapo, with a body like a bear and a head like a bucket. When a stranger lurks close—maybe

a drug person slinking toward the nearby train—
Guapo runs him off with deep growls and bites. Pure
fierceness like a wolf. With us he is just pure slobber
and licks. Guapo follows me sometimes to the milpita to hunt moles, but mostly he guards the house.

Our milpita, beautiful to me, lies not far from
a lonely stretch of railroad tracks. I have seen the
freight train. I have heard the shouts of the riders
atop it. And the screech of the wheels. I would like to
go close to watch. But when you are working in the
field you do not have time for train watching.

Both day and night, when a train passes this way,
I hear the whistle mourn and I think of the far places
it is going and I think of Toño who I love more than
anything. Gone four years. On the train. Now he
is nineteen.

When Mami got her sickness Toño raised me. He
and Abue. He is like my other father. But my brother
he is gone gone. Not ever will I see him again. For
me, it is a terrible train.

Really it is not one train, but many on many
routes, all going to the same place, la frontera, the
border. Here in this land of Oaxaca we call it La
Bestia, The Beast. Many people both children and
grown-ups struggle onto it to get away from this hard

life. Or gangs. Or to find loved ones lost in El Norte, Gringolandia. Some are chopped up right then and there if they miss the jump to get on. Many make it. But, mostly, like Toño, they never come back. Ay how I miss my hermano!

On this day I am walking barefoot behind Trini, up and down, up and down, plowing weeds in the furrows, the dirt rough beneath my feet. I dig my toes into it deep and feel a great surge of greenness inside myself, as though I were a growing plant.

The tall corn whispers as we go, about sky, about clouds, about secrets corn knows. The ox and I are both lost in the dust we make. Dust. Like the breath of the earth. *We are a little dust cloud of our very own*, I think as I walk. I am looking at nothing much. Then—Trini balks and plunges away dragging the plow, bellowing. "Trini!" I call, looking down for what has frightened him.

It is a body. Crumpled in the dust.

"Toño," I whisper, thinking my brother has come home. I hold my breath.

"Aggggh"—a small gasp comes from the body. Smaller than a whisper. Trembling, I bend down.

"Aggggh."

It is a boy. Younger than me. And he is bleeding. Bleeding bleeding into the dirt of our milpita. How could he get this far without help? The dust has settled upon him. This small dusty boy, he has lost one foot. I know without knowing The Beast has taken it.

"Papi! Abue!" I race for the house.

Abue with her herbs and chants and wisdom, she is a magical one. But I know as I run she can do nothing. Even so, we can comfort the broken boy. And we can pray.

The boy dies quickly. Here nobody knows him. He must have come from far away. Now he is buried with our prayers in the holy earth of the pueblo's graveyard, along with others of our family. Mami, and my brother and sister who lived only a few breaths. His blood has seeped into the furrows. Few know now his sleeping place but us, this boy taken by The Beast.

After this terribleness I think of Toño very much. He made The Beast journey alive. This is a great grace of God both Abue and Papi keep telling us. To find his mother, my friend Leo tried Beast Riding one time. He fell off. Now he walks with a cane. Leo is ten.

Every once in a while Toño sends money to help us. Little dribbles and bits, but no matter, it is money. Money he earns cleaning toilets in a big building and doing other throw-away jobs in a place called Los Angeles, The Angels for heaven sakes. How can the angels let my good brother work hard hard cleaning toilets, and for so little? He is smart. He has more school than I do. He should have a job of respect. But I know Toño like I know my shadow. Even with this mean work, he will do it with flare, maybe sometimes flourishing the toilet brush, maybe sometimes singing in his big, loud voice. I smile when I picture this.

I miss my brother and his smile and his flare. Two years ago he sent me his picture. He now has a mustache. Without him our family has a missing piece. My heart has a very big emptiness. The train that took Toño from us is the one that left the broken boy in the dust. The Beast. The very name makes me shake.

Our adobe is small. It is sheltered by two tired old trees and guarded by cactus. Tall and prickly soldiers. A bougainvillea has grown itself right over the roof, like a purple shawl. There is a yard noisy with chickens and one goat which chews everything including our clothing if we stand too close.

Our home has two rooms, one for cooking, one for sleeping. Since recently we have electricity, but it costs so much we use it little. Also, it works little, failing in storms, failing in earthquakes, failing because it just feels like it, I think. Electricity, it is a mystery. We use no light but candles at night. The bathroom is a hole dug in the earth outdoors. Sharing one bedroom on petates, palm mats, the five of us share snorings, sleepwalkings, nightmares, dreams.

Breakfast we eat together, to start the day as a family. Corn, chiles, frijoles, those are the Oaxaca foods. And eggs in some form. My favorite is with chopped-up chiles and nopales, cactus leaves carefully scraped free of thorns. And soft, warm tortillas or tlayudas, the big chewy ones. If I am not in school, Papi and I take lunches, mostly cheese and totopos, with us to wherever we are working. Each on his own. But in the evening always always we eat together gathered at our little wooden table that

Papi made. There, as we bow our heads over simple foods, Papi gives the blessing. He ends this by saying *Keep us happy with the small things*. And we are—I am anyway—happy with the small things of our life.

Abue believes that signs show themselves to guide our lives. She sees signs in the patterns of clouds or in how a tree holds out its arms or in a feather she has found. In the very face of the land. "Look for signs," she tells me when I ask where my life will take me. "Follow them."

One night on my petate, I dream. A pale figure rises, little clods of earth from the milpita soundlessly crumbling off the small body. The dead boy. Words, as if buried, come from the mouth. *I failed, but you—* A sign, as sure as anything!

I sit upright, shivering with the wonder of what I have seen. And the wonder of the words. Except for snuffles and peaceful breathings the room is quiet, all but my heart beating so loudly I believe it will wake everybody. But they stay sleeping. Through the little small window I see stars glimmering like promises in the dark. I can stand it no longer, not being with my brother who raised me. *I failed, but you—* The dead boy's words are showing the way. In this moment I make a decision. I choose out one star, the brightest. Trembling, I whisper to it in complete conspiracy. *Star, tell this to nobody, not a single soul. I am boarding The Beast. I am going to Toño.*

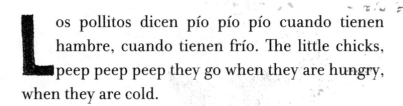

Los pollitos dicen pío pío pío cuando tienen hambre, cuando tienen frío. The little chicks, peep peep peep they go when they are hungry, when they are cold.

This day is dark. The sun is waiting to come up. The little ones, Belén and Javier, are still asleep. I am feeding the clucking chickens and singing a chicken song and plotting my journey to The Angels, Los Angeles. Where Toño is.

Since my dream of the nameless boy I have been plotting plotting. I must keep this secret close or Papi for certain will stop me. Not Abue. "We each must find our own way," she often tells me. She who sees signs in the way trees stand, in the forms of passing clouds. My sign now is the dead boy. In dreams he speaks to me. *I failed, but you—*

To leave, what I need are these things: food, warm clothing, money. What I have is this: nothing. Each day while I go about my chores my mind spins with plannings.

I begin to hoard foods. Small things that will not give me away. Stale or not one desperate day they will feed me. Mealtimes, instead of eating both my tortillitas, I stuff one into a pocket when I can, hoping that a hungry rat will not nose it out from its hiding place beneath my *petate*. Hoping also that my sharp-as-a-machete Papi will not nose it out even before rats do.

My Abue, smelling of the tortillas she makes, may know of my hidden supply. My Abue with her wise eyes and soul. These days sometimes she looks at me. Just looks. Showing neither sí or no. But I think she sees into my heart. I think there she sees Toño.

Another of my needs is dinero, money. What little we have goes for clothing and foods we do not grow ourselves. Café is a big money item. And azúcar. Ay how we all would love bundles of sugar. To make complete syrup of our café. But with sugar we are skimpers, even though.

I devise myself a peso plan, for the trip in general—food and stuff—but especially for my feet. I announce this foot part to my family in an offhand way. "The stones of the milpita are bruising my feet," I say. (Around this time I begin to limp, just slight slight, not drastically.) Of course my feet are like hog leather from these twelve mostly barefoot years of my life. My feet have known sandals, especially at school, for teacher respect. But they prefer to be free. I look down at them, as if they were utterly black and blue as a Oaxaca storm—and tender as new corn. Maybe I even whine, from the supposed pain. "I need tennis shoes" is how I end the scene. I cannot go barefoot on the train.

How can anybody of this tough and centuries-upon-this-land family believe such words? Such ridiculosities. I do not know. Maybe in this moment the angels of Los Angeles have gathered to watch over me. Or maybe more local angels. Anyway—a miracle!—my family agrees to shoes if any to fit me can be found.

If such tennis shoes exist I am to earn them. And I will. To do this thing I become Resolve itself.

Shoes for my journey. I know of a pair. And I will have them—if they are still there.

Abue says not a word about my sudden need for shoes. But her eyes, how they speak. I am certain she knows my thinking.

These shoes I have seen, they are in the tiendita, little store, of what we call the pueblito, our village of San Juan. San Juan is so small a place, on any day I believe I could nearly spit its whole complete length.

At the heart of it is the tiendita. Here is where flows all news. When a messenger finds us, here is where we come running to receive our rare phone calls from Toño. Most people here have cell phones, but we do not. Papi likes the old ways and the silence of the fields. Phone calls cost money, besides.

When Toño calls we dash to the little store, then pass the owner's cell phone around, all the family, and we talk fast fast as if to whoosh out everything to Toño in one breath. If I miss a phone call, I go off to be sad by myself.

The tiendita holds a collection of most beautifully disorganized items, both necessaries and "splurges for the soul," as Abue puts it. On the walls are calendars with pictures. And everywhere there are signs with prices for the great jumble of items waiting to be bought. Foods like frijoles and papas, clothing, plows, tools, nails, machetes, ropes, leather goods, baskets, comales for the toasting of tortillas and such, cleaning rags, buckets, and jeans jeans jeans, which have taken over. The tiendita has dulces, sweets. Like Pingüinos and Gansitos, both little cakes, which I stare at long long whenever I go in. Probably the little cakes are a bit hard from staleness, but they would still taste good. Now and then we splurge on them. And the smells! Raw sugar, cinnamon, honey, chile. Each time I enter the tiendita the whole big fragrance overcomes me, nearly lifts my feet from the floor. Inside myself I float.

One day I enter the tiendita with Abue. To seek shoes for my famously bruised feet. Some things have been waiting here so long, I believe, they have many layers of dust upon them. But one item does not have dust. The one I remembered. A pair of tennis shoes inside a glass case. White like clouds. *Beautiful like clouds*, I think. These cloud shoes, they speak to me as plain as anything. *Buy us. We will take you where you need to go. We will be faithful.* In this moment I feel that this is true.

They are not my size, but near enough. I will stuff them with paper to fit. The price is big. I bargain with the owner, Señora Crispina. We bargain bargain for a long time, back and forth, back and forth, till the cost is within my reach.

"Here is our trato, our deal," Señora Crispina announces. "At dawn each day you Manuel Flores will carefully sweep the sidewalk in front of the store. You will carefully sweep inside the store. And straighten signs and displays and set out new items for those that have been sold. All this you will do—very carefully—before school begins."

She smiles at me then, knowing that since Toño has gone I often wriggle myself from school early to help Papi.

"Could I sell cigarettes?" I ask with innocence, just to hear her fiery response.

"No, no, no, no, no!" she replies vigorously. She pops those "no"s out quickly like fiesta fireworks. "Cigarettes are no good. A boy should stay away from those."

So I will sweep sweep and straighten straighten. And soon, if the angels are gathered close, I will own cloud-white tennis shoes. The extra money will be mine. Of course I will give it to my family— all but some few pesitos which I will hold aside for my journey.

My last need: something of warmth if it becomes freezing on the back of The Beast.

Time passes. I measure it by the corn. We planted it some months ago. Now it is taller than me.

During all my plottings I could change my mind. I could stay to help my family. Or I could follow my now-obsession, to be with Toño. To get a job in Gringolandia to help out with money. My heart swings back and forth—yes, no, maybe so—till at last it settles upon yes.

Once Abue looks at me with love. She touches my face with her floury hands.

"You are our dreamer, Manuelito," she says to me in her starry voice, but with extreme seriousness. "Within you, you hold all of our dreams." That is all. Then she goes back to patting tortillas.

I hold their dreams. What does this mean?

One day I am the owner of tennis shoes. New ones. Cloud-colored ones. A miracle in itself. As I wriggle into them I think to myself about where they will take me. *Please*, I say to the tennies silently, *keep me on a good road always*. The tennies answer, *We will do our best.* My feet, they are completely happy with these shoes. They dance all by themselves, it seems, to show they are pleased. Of course the shoes will soon be dirty from dust of the milpita, but that is good. Maybe upon The Beast they will not be a quick thief-target.

One afternoon when I think Toño will be home, I make a secret call to him from the tiendita. So secret I take the cell phone outside, away from all listeners. "Hermano, brother," I say all in a rush when he picks up, "I am coming to you. If you tell Papi, I am coming anyway. I will call you when I can." I speak these words with such solemnness, I know Toño will keep still.

I keep up my tiendita work as long as I can, to add more to my little hoarded paper pesos. Not many, but they must do. For I am going now—after I get a sweater.

I have one, but I need a bigger one, to cover me when it is freezing atop The Beast. Papi's is the one I need. He would not give it to me for my unswerving purpose. He is generous in most ways, but not this. Already he has lost one boy to La Bestia. . . .

This night is quiet. The house is quiet. Its sleeping people are quiet. Quiet quiet to escape discovery I gather my few necessaries in a morral, a bag, including the tortillas and fresh chones, underwear. The phone numbers of the tiendita and of Toño. I have written them on little papers. These small papers I stuff into the pockets of my pants, along with my pesitos.

Just before I go, with great stealth I lift with care Papi's sweater from the hook where it hangs. I wrap it around me, his too-big sweater with many holes. Papi's torn old sweater wraps around me like his very arms. It smells of Papi and gives me courage to leave.

Now I am a thief.

I stand outside the door of my home.

I lift a hand in adiós.

Maybe I have tears. I do not know. I am numb.

Suddenly Guapo is beside me. Quiet quiet. Smart dog. Like Abue he knows I am going. He knows not to bark, not to whine, not to follow me. Only the grillos are singing as I bend to pet dear Guapo's big-as-a-bucket head. Only the crickets sing me away. Into the dark. Toward The Beast.

walk in the dark with the grillos for company and
the sweep of stars overhead.

I am alone.

I am afraid.

Will I make it onto The Beast?

Or will I die this night?

Ay Jesús what will become of me?

I hurry to where The Beast will stop, a thing I have
learned from listening to talk in the tiendita. The
stars help me find the way. I crouch as I go, suddenly
certain that Papi is following me. One ancient street

lamp is trying to light this lonely place, sputtering its life away. I shrink back from the light, hiding from imagined-Papi.

I hear The Beast roar before I see it. I feel its great terribleness. I smell the reek of creosote, the stuff that soaks the railroad ties. I smell the weeds along the tracks. I smell my own fear.

The night is cold. I wrap Papi's sweater tight about me, the sweater with his scent. I grip tighter the morral with my food and pat the places where I have hidden the precious phone numbers and pesitos. These I hope—and the angels—will get me to Toño.

The Beast screeches to a stop in this alone spot. From here, so close, it is bigger, darker, more frightening than the thing I have seen faraway in the distance. All of metal. Crusted with dust and grime. And horrible. A chill shivers through my whole body, like the chill of death.

There are others like me here, strangers, hiding from police who will try to stop them. Waiting, I guess, for the thing to start up again. I barely notice them, so fixed am I on this terrible train.

Before now, in the pueblito, I have asked questions with my best casualness about this train. Has anybody here ridden it? Are there polis, police? What are the secrets? What must I know to last? I tried to ask Leo, my crippled friend, but he was scared silent by his Beast experience. Still, I have learned poco a poco, little by little. But I have made one big mistake. I failed to ask, when it gets going at a big speed, how do I scramble on without losing an arm or a leg? How to get on without dying.

So here am I. Here is The Beast come alive again with a roar. Already moving faster and faster. What now? I am paralyzed with indecision. Frozen. But I must this moment jump on.

Suddenly, magically, I see shapes emerging from the tops of the cars, from the sides, from myriad hidden places. People viajando de mosca, traveling like a fly. Hanging on however they can. Dark shapes like mushrooms spontaneously arising, arms flailing, signaling me what to do. A wild chorus of voices, a complete cacophony—not soft grillos—shouts crazily from everywhere it seems, urging me forth. *Oye, chavo, grab the ladder in front! Grip tight for all you are worth! Do not slip! No, no, no! Not the back! One false step and the wheels, they will chew you up! Come on, come on, it is passing you, órale, hurry, jump on!*

My head is buzzing. The Beast is racing fast like a panther. The brotherhood of Beast Riders is lifting me in a huge hum of instructions, with great ferocity of purpose, with a kind of love new to me. Love that says *Stranger, we are in this together.*

In this moment I am inside the hum. I listen to everything of this most marvelous noise. Mostly I hear *The ladder in front!* So I aim for that. I am running alongside The Beast. Running running at the flank, panting. I must move now or be dragged in the gravel and left behind.

The front! The front! The ladder! The riders keep shouting. The wheels churn, as if grinding this tip out, again and again.

I look up.

I grab hold of a ladder.

Wheel sparks burn my arm.

I mumble a prayer.

And I leap.

IV

A miracle. I am aboard The Beast.

At first, by the ladder, I swing in the wind, my body thumping the metal car that I cling to. Next thing, I heave myself up and am on top, thumped all round with bravos by other riders. They are grubby and stinking of sweat and urine and filth, and prickly with beards, like cactus—except the women and children—but I do not care. I like cactus.

There is nothing to hold on to so I cling to any-body I can, seeking a place to sit. Nothing is still. Nothing is safe. I crouch to keep my balance. The Beast lurches. My stomach lurches. I pray I will not fall off and be sliced to pieces.

One man must see my fear. "Here!" He shouts and squeezes some room for me. The train noise is so terrible, you always must shout.

We are squashed together, gripping each other, on top of The Beast. Our smells, our breaths, our fears, mingling. Many grip the sides also, by ladders. The thing churns on its way, roaring as it goes, careening sometimes side to side like a drunken dragon, leaning, nearly tipping I think with horror, always screaming, while the wind hurls itself over the long and mourning monster. *A–hoooooooo!*

Soot from the engine fills my mouth, blankets my clothes, sifts down my neck. When I spit, my spit is black. Already I want a bath.

Apart from the brotherhood of riders here, there is also here a brotherhood of rateros, thieves, swarming The Beast like rats. And gangs of asesinos. Preying on others' misery. These would kill in a finger snap for one single tortilla. Or for nothing. They would maul me for my pesitos, then how would I get a phone card to call my home, or Toño?

I have heard these things in the tiendita. Now I learn them for real. Suddenly a voice comes from close close.

"So what do we have here?" says the guy, his eyes burning at me, and laughing in a most ugly way. "¿Un pollito?" A chick?

Apart from The Beast itself, I feel more fear leaking into my heart. So soon a thief! This one, with weasel eyes, if he was cold he would burn his own grandmother to make a fire, I believe.

I can hardly speak. But finally I struggle out in answer, "You have a Flores," gathering my family name up for courage.

"Flowers!" The guy roars with evil. "A ramo of roses! How sweet!"

He has friends who jeer along with him, as if he is the boss. My heart is thundering as with his grubby hands he roughs me up. Inside myself I shriek, *Toño!* But I am a Flores, so into the night not a peep do I make.

"He is a boy. Leave him be." An ice voice speaks.

The thieves and I turn to see a thin man appear from nowhere, one who looks like he is made all of wire. He is the grubbiest person I have ever seen, his skin dark with the dirt of years it seems. His eyes, deep green, are as cold as his voice, and look ancient ancient, as though he has traveled this earth since

time and time. In his hand he holds a machete—
blade bitten from who knows what terrible deeds—
which gleams with the light of the stars.

My attackers must feel like I do about this guy.
That he is from some Otherwhere.

"Okay okay," the boss-one mumbles. He and his
pals slink away. Nimble as rats they jump from car to
car, into the deepening dark. And I am left alone with
this cold personage holding the machete. Even in
Papi's sweater, I shiver. I grasp The Beast, balancing
the best I can. And I hold my breath, believing in
spite of his words to those bad ones that this guy
may be Death.

"I am Gabriel" is all he says.

"I am Manuel," I whisper. "Gracias."

"Come, let us eat." His eyes now hold a
kindly look.

My terror melts—mostly.

"I have tortillitas," I say, still finding my breath.
I look for my bag, to share with him.

It is not here. I look up again, horrified. "I am
sorry," I say bleakly, "I can give you nothing. My
food, it is gone."

"That maldito with his pawing hands, he has stolen my tortillitas!" I pat my pockets quickly and feel only the little phone numbers. In my panic the words burst out. "Also he got my pesitos!" I shout. When The Beast stops I cannot buy food. Or water. What will I do?

I must sound wild with worry for Gabriel at once calms me.

"Fear not, Manuel. I have food."

So atop The Beast, while I struggle to stay on, we eat. Cold beans and rice. And it is good. Inside myself, like Papi would, I give thanks.

"Your age?" Gabriel asks.

"Twelve." For politeness reasons I do not dare ask his age. But I think it is in the thousands.

"A runaway?"

I realize suddenly this is true. All I say is, "I am going to find my brother."

"Ah," says Gabriel, his ancient eyes boring into me. "Brothers, they are a pull. They tug at the heart."

Suddenly, I feel tired tired. And achy from the shaking of The Beast. I want desperately to sleep, but the dead boy ghosts into my mind once more. I have a deep fear of falling to the tracks. I struggle to keep awake. I sway.

"Sleep," says Gabriel in his chopped speech. "I will see that you do not fall." He is hunched in such a way that beneath his shirt his thin shoulder blades have a certain lumpy look. In my exhaustion I wonder stupidly, *Wings?*

I must be out almost at once, sleeping deep like a fallen tree. In dreams I think of chiles and beans, and home. I see the faces of my family. In dream-thoughts I wonder, *Will I ever see them for real again?*

When I awake Gabriel has vanished.

The stars too have fled to somewhere else. Like watery ink, the dark is now thinned.

Where am I? I wonder at first, still drugged with sleep. *Are we there yet?* I ask myself with hope.

I find myself tied with a rawhide cord to a small pole at the end of the train car. So that I stay on top of The Beast. Careful not to fall, I untie the cord and place it in a pocket of Papi's sweater. For when I sleep. One last kindness from Gabriel. With that thought comes a clench of my stomach. Now I must look out for myself.

Lying there I listen carefully to the sounds that wrap round me like a shawl—the laughings, the cryings, the songs, the prayers of the many voices of the people bunched so close. I listen also to the loud train sounds. And I remember something I learned in school, a trabalenguas, tongue twister, with lots of *r*s: Rápido rápido corren los carros sobre los rieles del ferrocarril. Fast fast race the train cars over the rails of the train. I say this over and over above the noise, to calm my fears.

The Beast rushes through the land. On the way I try to make myself look sympathetic, so that people as poor and desperate as I am will give me food and protection. A tip from Toño when Papi was not near the phone: *Because you are young they will help you.* It shames me to do this, but it is the only way. Now that I have no money, eyes pleading and big, I beg.

We pass milpitas, and big spiky maguey plants with white sheets and colorful laundry drying upon them. Heart stabs of my home! I imagine those who wash our clothing and bedding then carefully drape it over magueys to dry. Once Mami and Abue, now Abue alone. All of a sudden I feel a big sadness, so far from my family.

I am on a strange train bound for a strange land, among strangers, many from far places, with nobody who truly cares for me. I Manuel Flores am on my own.

The wheels scream and the wheels scream and things happen. I Manuel Flores am wrapped in the unholy noise and wind from this unholy train.

Soon the motion of The Beast feels different. It is slowing! A stopping place is coming with big buildings—and polis with fierce dogs that can smell even fear. This I have heard at home. And here also, from other riders. If I am caught I will be sent back. I cannot face that.

Knowing they have customers clinging to The Beast, suddenly vendors burst forth from nowhere, selling tortas, cacahuates, chips, bottled water, Coca-Colas, diapers, soap, you name it. But right now nobody cares about vendors. Everybody swarms for the ladders in a crazed rush to evade the police.

Somebody nearby shouts at me, "Chavo, the moment you can, scramble down a ladder!"

And another, "Run fast for the bushes!"

"Duck down! Do not move!"

"Quick! Follow me!"

The faithful tennis shoes and I make a dash for it.

Next thing I am crashing through brambles, patches of briars, being lashed, stifling my cries against the whips of wicked branches. Then I squat behind a bush, panting panting. While the polis beat every plant in sight and shout, I crouch with the guy who called for me to follow.

I have planned so carefully. I have only started my trip. I cannot get caught so soon. In this moment this is what I think.

I am not caught by polis or dogs, not this time, but by this man who has tricked me. A hard lesson. With no sound, but with a big yank he snatches my sweater with the rawhide cord and the smell of Papi. Before he bounds away he yells, "Trusting fool! You will never reach the border!"

Inside myself I say, *The little chicks, peep peep peep they go when they are hungry, when they are cold.*

VI

I feel blood. Mine. Sticky. On my face and arms. They sting from the slashes of the branches. But I cannot clean my wounds. I have no water.

When I was little and I got the slightest injury, Mami, Papi, Abue, Toño—whoever was closest— patted my hurt and said to me this: Sana, sana, colita de rana, si no sanas hoy, sanarás mañana. Get well, get well, little frog tail. If you do not get well today, you will tomorrow. There is nobody to sana, sana me now.

>>>>>>>>>>

You never know when The Beast will come alive again, I have learned, so you should not go into the cities. You have to stay close to the tracks. You may wait for hours and hours. The signal is when you hear the clanks of the cars linking up. That says The Beast once more, with a jolt, is leaving.

A train is leaving right now. I hear the link-ups. So must everybody else for they all run to jump on again. The wheels begin screaming. Then out surge hidden police, their big dogs straining on leashes, lunging for people and barking.

"¡Alto! ¡Alto!" The polis yell. "Stop! Stop!"

But nobody does. While the train gains speed everybody rushes for the ladders and scrambles for a safe place where they cannot be grabbed and forced back from their goal of El Norte.

This is not the same train as before, and it is not so crowded. But still it is on the same tracks. Different people have scrambled aboard. Different Beast Riders with their many hopes. If they could take the bus they would. But buses cost . . . Looking out for each other as best we can, the unspoken Brotherhood goes north.

I make it to a boxcar top, but one guy near me does not. His pant leg is ripped by the teeth of a police dog, not as fierce as my Guapo back home, but scary-fierce anyway. The teeth clamp the man's leg like a trap and he is bleeding bleeding. He screams frantically and tries to break free. But he cannot escape.

"¡Socorro! Help me!" He yells and yells. The poli yanks his straining dog back from the too-close train. Somebody reaches down for the man's hand and begins to pull him up. But he is too weak. The leg . . .

He slips down down, to be eaten alive by The Beast.

Now The Beast is gone from there. And the torn man? Who knows? A vision of the boy who died in our milpita comes to me. I lie on my panza, belly, on the boxcar, trembling. For a long time, in my deep heart, I hear the moans of the boy, I hear the cries of the man.

In our village my friends and I used to shout a gruesome goodbye. ¡Adiós! ¡Que te vaya bien! ¡Que te machuque el tren! ¡Que te remuela bien! Go well! May the train smash you! May it grind you up well!

Never will I say that again.

As The Beast roars on, my wounds become warm. I feel a throbbing. Already, I believe, they are festering. I must do something for that. Even though I know there is nothing there but the too-small-to-steal phone numbers, I dig my hands into my pockets.

What is this? I feel something strange in one, something brittle and crumbly wrapped in paper. In my panic at being robbed, I missed it. I pull out a pinch and look at it. But it is not the looks that give it away, it is the sweet scent. I was right. All along Abue knew my plan. She has hidden here a curing herb for me. When my journey began the leaves must have been whole. Their dust will help me still.

Along with the curing leaves there is a note. *Hold on to my hand even when I have gone away from you.* And I do. Ever ever I hold on to Abue's hand.

"Water, please," I beg from a lady nearby, pointing to my angry scratches. I need water also to drink. My thirst is great. By now I know that Beast Riders, mostly they help each other. And she helps me. With a look of concern, from a plastic bottle she pours precious water into a small empty can. I sip this gift, slow slow. Water is hoarded gold.

What I do not drink I guard carefully. When the sun heats it, I sprinkle in some of Abue's precious herb crumbs. I touch the hot leaf paste to my face, my arms. "Que Dios la bendiga," I say to the lady. I whisper a prayer of gracias to my Abue. And to Dios.

I am grateful that I will be healed. Still, I fear that at night the cold will get to me. Hot days. Cold nights. What will I do with no sweater?

While plowing our milpita I have often watched beetles in the fields. These are the ruedacacas, rollers of dung. Their one big concern is caca. As soon as Guapo or Trini shits, the ruedacacas are there, gathering the warm dung. Rolling it into marble-size balls, then moving it with their small might toward their far tunnels. I love to see them working, so faithful to the task. Sometimes I pause just to study their toilings. I know I should keep on in my own toilings, but these beetles are so enchanting.

If they have success and roll the caca home, all year they can feed upon caca balls. If they lose it, or it is stolen by another beetle, they will have none. But always always they keep laboring. Seeking out dung. Fighting for some, the precious popó. Rolling rolling the dung. That is the way of the ruedacacas.

Here am I on this terror train thundering to The North. I am hungry. I am thirsty. I am tired. I am scared. I am wounded. Though crushed against many other people, I am lonely to the bone. In this moment I want to quit. To stop someplace. Anyplace. Then somehow struggle myself home. But then I imagine the lowly ruedacacas, working working. They become my example. I feel my spirit rise. I have good new resolve. Like the ruedacacas, I will keep going.

Dimmest dawn. January is fleeing away. This day, in my deep heart I *feel* it is my birthday. For my best wish I would be with my family. Though I am too old for such a thing, I wish for a piñata to comfort me. A little donkey. Blue. Like when I was young. For all my strong wishings, these things do not happen. With nothing, I turn thirteen.

Long scary days and nights flow one into another. I think of home. How I would love to call my family, but I have no money. And I fear their dear voices would convince me to return.

Now Abue will be patting out the tortillas of desayuno, breakfast. Now Papi will be trailing Trini through the furrows because I am not there. And little Belén and Javier will be doing my chores for me. Guilt grabs my heart.

I clutch the lurching spine of The Beast. Night and day, people—dirty, sweaty, hungry, thirsty, scared like me—press against each other, people from all over. They sprawl on whatever space there is and pray. To stay on, to keep warm, I lean against others huddled there. They lean against me. Sometimes it is freezing. Sometimes the heat is of ten thousand devils. Nights, I hug myself against the cold. I rub my injured arms to try to keep warm.

When I look at the faces of these other riders, I see tiredness, loneliness, sadness. As though the light has gone out of them. I wonder, *Has it also gone from me?*

Always I watch for gangs, I try to keep from falling from the train, I search for any speck of shade—

to keep from shriveling up and becoming a momia, like a Guanajuato mummy, so famous. I dare not enter a boxcar for fear of somebody slamming the door. In the heat I would cook in there.

We riders of The Beast try to blink ourselves awake. But if we cannot, we guard each other. The worst thing is to fall asleep and be attacked—or fall off. I am filthy beyond filthy, both soot- and sweat-covered. Apart from family and food, what I most long for is a bath.

With the steady roar of The Beast, I become less watchful for danger—or maybe just more exhausted. Whichever it is, one evening when I am darting from a hiding place back toward The Beast, two shots whine by my head. I freeze. I am captured by a poli.

VII

This poli has no big-tooth dog, but alone he is scary enough. A bulk bristling with weapons.

His huge fists keep bunching and unbunching, as if getting set to hit me. Instead he drags me to the police station, kicking me and spitting out bad words like bullets, probably angry that I have nothing he can steal.

"¡Pendejo! ¡Idiota! ¡Cabrón!" Words we would never say at home. Ours is not a bad-word family.

When this guy has hurt me enough, he orders me back to where I come from. The milpita. The time I will lose! And the spirit to go on! For sometimes my urge to go home, it is great, though not as great as my need for Toño. In these weak moments, I think of the ruedacacas, never quitting their toiling. In my head I say, *I am never quitting my goal.*

Besides, I cannot leave my dear ones again. It would be a heart-tearing thing. So I do not go home, but to a nearby village of no consequence. I have no idea where I am. The trees are different here than the few we have. I do not know their names. And there is not so much cactus. I hope I am close to the border, but truly I do not know.

I must find food. On The Beast I have begged and been fed. Still, with many meals missed, my bones—like those of a starving animal—are nearly poking through my skin. And with thirst my tongue is dry as a dead leaf. I am cramped with hunger. So here I go begging from house to house.

"Do you have a little food? A little water?" I ask humbly at one place.

"We have little enough for ourselves, you nasty boy!" The lady yells. "Go away!"

She slams the door so hard, the ground shivers where I stand.

I go on.

"A little something? I am hungry."

I am turned away.

By nightfall I am ferociously hungry. Dizzy. And thirsty. Feeling desperate. When I find water in a ditch, I strain it through my ragged shirt and drink drink. Then I keep going. Finally I come upon a garbage heap, outside of a cantina. The reek of the mound is great, and at first though my belly is empty, I retch. Others, maybe Beast Riders like me, are already scrounging there for bones, moldy fruit, anything. Dogs like skeletons are also nosing nosing. And rats.

Suddenly a poli strides up, to arrest us, I think, sending a panic-ripple through me. I tense to run. But he seems not to have the heart for this. He just walks on. A poli with a heart! Ay!

Some people try to scare me away, to keep these few scraps for themselves. But I persist. I find enough food, though a little bit rotten, to get me through this day. This night I give gracias for the little I have found.

I wonder, *Like a rat did Toño on his journey eat garbage also?* I know he did.

With no pesitos I must find work. Next day, again, I ask for food. I look and look for work. At last, when the sun is high and everybody is enjoying

47

lunch—everybody but people like me—I beg once more, in a cracked voice. One man takes pity and says softly, "Pásale." Come in.

After the time on The Beast, with so many rateros, I trust nobody, at least not at first. I hang back in case the man pounces upon me for the little he imagines I have. Or turns me in. I am ready to run.

I have learned to read people—friend or enemy—by their eyes. But this guy is standing so that I cannot see his. After all, I do not need to see them, for there is a goodness-shimmer surrounding him. This man he knows I am starving, for, when we are inside his small kitchen, without a word he offers a taco from his own plate. And water. *Bless him*, I say in my heart. I give him gracias—also to God—and try not to eat like a wolf.

The next thing I get is a bath. Oh to be clean again!

This quiet-voiced man is Señor Santos, I soon discover, whose wife has recently died. A small, round person with a big, round laugh, neat in all ways, he is a maker of tejas, roof tiles, the kind I sometimes helped Papi make. To keep our house whole when wind and rain and sun crumbled the old ones. Or they, from tiredness, slid off. Few people make their own tiles anymore, but Señor Santos still does. He wants to put a part of himself into each one, I believe.

Señor Santos gives me a job as his tejas helper. He gives me also a cot to sleep on and a fresh shirt and chones and a sweater. When I pull it on I think of Papi and I force away tears. These items, their cost will be taken from my pay. My old pants I keep. I can use them still, till they get more holes. A bed! Clean clothing! Money! Miracles and miracles and miracles!

This man, when I am clean from a bath, he appears. Armed with scissors. With absolute purpose he goes for my hair. After many whackings and mumblings, he circles round me, clicking the still-hungry scissors in the air, pulling, poking, checking his work.

"Ha!" cries Señor Santos, admiring the result, "You no longer resemble a boy of the wild."

I am proud to work beside him. He teaches me what he knows. Mostly the proper way to mix the clay, the proper way to form the tiles and smooth the dry ones, so that through wind, sun, rain they will last and last. "With care," he tells me, "this is the proper way. Your work—in even the smallest things—it is a mirror of you."

I do not tell him that Papi has taught me all this. It does not hurt to learn good lessons twice.

At the end of each day, we leave the tiles we have made stacked against each other, ready to bake in tomorrow's sun. Sometimes in the night a rooster or a cat walks upon a damp tile and leaves its track, like signing its name. The track is baked into the tile. It says *I am a rooster. I was here.* I love that.

When we enter his home, Señor Santos and I both smell like red clay. A good and honest smell. I do not hurry to bathe it away.

When I am at work making tejas and coated with the red clay and dust under the good warm sun, again I think of Papi. And the roof which we repaired often, together. I think of him when I bend a piece of clay over my knee to form a tile in the olden way. I enjoy seeing my work, a mirror of me, tile upon tile stacked up, knowing that the shape of my knee will one day give shelter to somebody.

With my savings I get a telephone card, to phone home. In town Señor Santos helps me buy one and helps me make my call.

Since last I spoke with my family, many things have happened. My life has changed. I have changed. My voice has changed. I no longer fear that their dear voices will pull me home. For my resolve to go on is stronger. But now I worry about something else. Will they recognize me or hang up? I am so excited to talk with them I can barely stand still. I try to think what I will say. I will not have much time.

"Cálmate, cálmate, little grasshopper," says Señor Santos gently, watching me jump around.

I try to calm down, but simply cannot. I dig into my pocket for the telephone numbers so important to me. The one link with my family. My heart drops suddenly like a rock. The little papers with the numbers, they are not there!

VIII

The tiendita phone number has been stolen. And Toño's. I am holding a phone card in my hand, but I cannot call home. I feel myself lost in the world, like a feather floating floating.

I think again. Maybe I somehow lost them myself. From a torn pocket. The wind? But then I worry that they will be found. A bad one could call my family and lie that I am captive and demand ransom. From my family who has not a pesito to spare. My family who has only themselves and dirt and corn.

"What is it?" asks Señor Santos, his voice with deep concern.

"Their telephone number, it is gone."

"Cálmate, cálmate," he says again. "There must be something we can do."

He is like that, he says "we."

In my mind, in this moment I see a dung beetle, working with all its small might. I start working my brain with all that I can. I think. I think. Then—the number it is *not* gone. My time in school comes back to me. And the teacher who called me "Manuelito Memorizer." The number has been here in my head all along. Toño's also.

I make the call. I know that Señora Crispina, of the tiendita, sends somebody running running for my family. We all sound as excited as grasshoppers. First thing they say: "You are well?" First thing I say: "*Sí.*" They pass the phone like a hot tamal and I speak to everybody. All of us are older. But all the love is still there. Stronger. They will pass my news to Toño. I will call Toño when I am closer to him. Fast fast we speak. Then our voices become full of tears, and slower, as if to hold on to each other. The hardest part is saying adiós. Before they go, they sing me "Las mañanitas," the birthday song.

For today is my birthday. I did not say this to Señor Santos. It would give me pena, embarrassment. As if I were asking for a fiesta. And for somebody to be with joy that I was born. Like a child, I wish for a piñata like I always had before. A little donkey. Blue. A little blue donkey piñata does not appear. It does not matter. I know my family is with joy that I was born.

I have stayed in this place of safety for far too long. I have to keep going. Toño is in The Angels, waiting. My savings are enough now to travel on. But I do not leave without telling Señor Santos my plan and thanking him. This man who gave me a place in his home. Nearly a year I have stayed with him. Nearly a lifetime, it seems.

The evening I go, the grillos are singing their creaking song. I remember when I left home. I close my eyes to imagine the voices of those I left behind. I imagine I hear corn shuffling in wind. My heart tugs to go there, but Toño's tug is stronger.

Señor Santos and I, we share un abrazo.

"I will always remember you."

"And I you, Manuelito. Que Dios te bendiga."

"Que Dios lo bendiga a usted," I say to him.

Truly I hope that God will bless always this kind and noble man—and me.

I turn and slip into the pocket of the dark.

IX

On my way again. Since leaving Señor Santos I have been heading for The North, always always. Heading for another place along The Beast route. Another place to jump aboard.

It is night. In the distance I hear the growl of The Beast. I am older now. Tougher. Wilier. Still the train sound brings back my fears. I do not know what lies ahead. Blending into the dark—mouse gray, mouse still—as The Beast approaches I bunch myself to jump.

I am not wily enough. Before I spring, instead I am sprung upon. Ambushed and dragged away from the tracks. Away from the other hidden riders. Just days since I left Señor Santos's place of safety! My blood freezes. My heart forgets to beat, then bangs crazily. A pack of men. Animals all. A famous gang, famous for drugs and liquor. About five of them armed with many rough old-time weapons, mainly machetes to hack you up, surround me. I know them right off, by their black T-shirts that blare, LOS BANDIDOS. Toño warned me.

I twist from the filthy grasp of one, only to be snared by his comrade, his grip as fierce as my dog Guapo's jaws. Like a stringy rooster I am tougher than I look, but not tough enough to fight all of them.

"A rabbit!" one of them shouts in a drunken way. "Let's roast it."

Inside I quaver like a crouched rabbit, but, as before on The Beast, I do not show it. I am a Flores.

Toño told me that these guys work for the police for privileges and for part of what those guarros rob from Beast Riders. They also steal on their own. And when they catch somebody . . . I begin to sweat.

"Good idea," one snarls with evil bravado. "Start the fire."

And they do. First they plunge around in the dark, shuffling and cursing, grabbing up leaves and sticks, lurching, stumbling all over the place because of the liquor they have been drinking. Their breath. How it reeks.

One is guarding me, striking me, stomping me, raining punches down upon me, grinning all the while in a crazed and chilling way. I look wildly around. There is no escape. Though I have tried hard to hide it, by now I must smell of fear. I *am* afraid. Sorely.

A small fire is crackling. These devils are laughing, their murderous eyes burning down at me. They are holding me so that I cannot squirm, shoving into my face a hot branding iron. I call up my family, all the people of Flores, to give me bravery. I clench my teeth tight tight. *I will not whine for mercy. I will not bleat out my fear. I will not scream.* I clench so hard, I feel a tooth crack. I pray as never before.

"Look, cabrón." The vicious leader says, all slurry. "With this brand, you will be of a gang too. The mangy, scraggy, sorry gang of Beast Riders."

They bark like mad dogs as four pin me down. "You will not crush me!" I shout. I twist and lash out with full-blown fury. But no matter my wild thrashings, with relish the loco leader slowly presses the brand into my hand. I hear the skin sizzle. I smell the smell of my own flesh melting. I do not cry out, though there is searing pain. Pain beyond pain. Then nothing.

When finally I wake up I am in a daze and wonder what has befallen me. I feel as though my blood has drained away. Barely breathing, I wait to die in the dirt where they have dumped me. At last, when I struggle to open my eyes, I can open only one. The other is swollen shut. From the good eye I see a blurred form. One of my captors is crouching to finish me! I groan and urge my body to flee. But crumpled there in the dust of the road I can barely move. The taste of blood is strong in my mouth. My teeth. My tongue tells me one of them is gone. My whole bloodied self, it is throbbing.

The guy squats so close I can feel his breath. I curl up and try to cover my head, waiting for a machete chop to come.

Instead comes a soft whisper, "*Shhhh, shhhh.*" Slowly I try to focus. The person before me is not a savage, but a woman. "*Shhhh, shhhh.*" She cradles me like a baby.

Out of my throat comes a wheeze.

"Abue, am I dead?" I mumble, believing my grandmother is with me now. Even to mumble costs me.

"Not one bit," the woman says caringly.

"With all gentleness," she instructs while she and others lift me. It seems from the little I can grasp, I am not a dead one—just very broken.

Like dust devils, those evil ones passed quickly through my life. This woman, she stays. Little by little I learn from her what has happened. Mine is no sana, sana situation. The gang of brutes, they beat me insensible, till nearly my whole body turned blue. They gashed my face. Injured one eye. They cracked my skull and broke four ribs and one leg. Also some toes. The doctor himself is not yet certain of the number. All I feel is pain pain.

They took my belongings—the faithful tennis shoes, my clothes—everything but my chones. In the palm of one hand they branded me with a crude horned B. A B that stands for their gang name, LOS BANDIDOS. To show how they hurt people. But for me and I am sure for many others who have suffered from them, the в means something else. A badge of pride. All my life—if I recover—all I meet who know this dreaded train, when they see the brand, will know who I am: Manuel Flores, Beast Rider.

X

I am broken but unbroken. Bones sí, spirit no.

The doctor is unsure of what the treatment should be. In a haze I hear him, them, whispering. He and Serafina, my protector. The one who found me.

Having heard me, out of my head, babbling telephone numbers, they have already passed news of me to my family. I would love to talk with them, but I can barely speak. Ay how they will worry! Ay how they will pray! Ay the mystery words they will say for my recovery! My Abue, she will for certain share with Serafina her remedies—which herbs are the most useful, the most potent, the most prized for this work before them. The work of keeping me undead.

"Where to begin," says the doctor in a hollow tone. I believe he has not had this sort of experience.

"Do not worry," Serafina says calmly, tending to me like the mother hen of the pollitos song. "I know the cure."

"What?"

"Soup."

The doctor attempts to repair the breaks. Serafina, her goal is bigger.

Serafina believes strongly in the power of pumpkin-flower soup. From a recipe, old old, she brews this molten gold. Spoon by spoon, bowlful by bowlful, over the next months, Serafina hovering close, I sip a soup of pumpkin flowers. And certain healing teas which bring comfort. As I become stronger, I can think—a little—and when I take the soup, a glorious color, I consider my golden insides. Then, weakly, I smile, thinking of home, where my people would also care tenderly for me.

My life becomes one long groan of pain. During these days, in visions or dreams, scenes of home float up to me. One time we are eating Abue's fresh tortillas, warm warm. All seated at our table so small our elbows are nearly touching. Saying grace. Papi is saying "Keep us happy with the small things." His theme. Oh to touch elbows—just to be in the little room—with them.

Once, in a vision, instead of working, I am lazing in a soft furrow of our milpita, gazing up into the endless sky at a hawk. Once I see a candle at our window. A nub. The candle has been blown out. All are asleep for the night. Then, by magic, the candle lights by itself. Once also I dream of Toño. I awake. Urgently I say into the dark, "You must get to him. You must get to your brother."

How many cauldrons of this beautiful soup does it take to bring me back to life? A number I cannot count. For certain the pumpkin flowers do their work, but I believe it is the love of Serafina and the many good souls of this dusty village and God that makes me once more whole.

While I am near death, each day, I learn little by little that villagers come. They chant. They sing. They light candles. They pray. They hold my hand—not the raw, bandaged one. Some only stand by my bed and wait.

And the love takes hold.

I begin to heal.

One day Serafina brings her golden cure, then sits beside me while I sip. We do not speak. Then, in a thin slot in the quiet, she leans and gently touches my head. "Mi viejito," she says with the voice of a mother. My old man. I must look puzzled for she then brings a mirror, cracked but good enough. There is my solemn reflection looking back at me, my hair as white as salt.

From my experiences my hair has been frightened and gone white. Now everybody calls me El Chavo Viejo, The Old Kid.

To celebrate my recovery Serafina presents me with new clothing and a new pair of tennis shoes. I mourn my first ones, faithful to the end but stolen. "These are to keep safe your feet," she says, unveiling them with her usual resolve. I know she means that they are to keep safe my whole self. So I can move more easily upon my journey. She knows that this stop with her is just a rest.

As I grow stronger I grow inquieto, restless. I look for something to do. Limping along in the new tennis shoes, I take walks, at first small ones, then longer. And the little children, they follow me. They take turns, but always, one holds on to my good hand. Maybe they think I will fall. Or become lost. Or wander off for my faraway home. The children. I believe that they think I need them. I do.

When we are not walking, I teach the little ones things of my childhood so far in the past. They learn the song of the pollitos, a song of chocolate, the train chant. From their many fallings and scrapings, already they know the chant of sana, sana. Even when it is not yet night, I sing to them the lullaby that Mami sang to me:

Duérmete mi niño,
Duérmete mi sol,
Duérmete pedazo
De mi corazón.

Sleep, my child.
Sleep, my sun.
Sleep, little piece
Of my heart.

Mami. My mother who gave me light. When I sing this my voice breaks into pieces. Also my heart.

So. With the children I sing songs. I walk. My white hair is a wonder to them. They want to touch it.

"It is okay?" they say, like my hair is a thing of magic.

"It is okay," I answer, leaning down for them to reach. What a thing. To feel their small hands upon my head, it is a kind of blessing.

Sometimes I sweep the church. Not with big energy. Small sweepings, broom-whisperings.

Then, one day, I am almost my old self. My hair will ever be white. One eye will always droop. Always I will walk with a limp. Always my brand will say my story. But after nearly one year by Serafina's calendar and the vigilance of Dios—and uncountable pots of soup—I am recovered.

To leave these people. It is a wrench. But Toño is in Los Angeles. Like the ruedacacas, I must keep going. Everybody of this place has given to me, and given again. I have nothing to give in return. Serafina, the doctor, the villagers, the niños, ever after, each one will stay always always in my prayers.

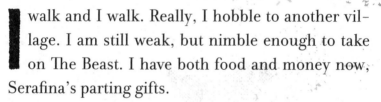

XI

I walk and I walk. Really, I hobble to another village. I am still weak, but nimble enough to take on The Beast. I have both food and money now, Serafina's parting gifts.

I listen for the *reeench* of wheels, a whistle-scream. Signs that The Beast is coming. Maybe this will be my last stretch on the train. Serafina said that to my dream I am close close.

I have been told where to wait. In time, with a great hiss of hot breath, The Beast stops in this place. Once again I am hiding close by in the tall weeds, awaiting my chance to haul myself up when the wheels begin to grind and screech, when once more it begins to race.

I look at the horned B burned into my palm. Beast Rider. Instead of raising fear, the small brand gives me power.

It is daylight. A bad time to try this. People are milling along the tracks, waiting for something in this poorest of poor places. Some carry clubs. To stop me and the other riders?

Another beating. In spite of my brand, a pulse of panic grabs me. I nearly turn back.

"What are they waiting for?" I whisper to a fellow Beast Rider.

"Us."

From imagined blows I cringe.

"To help us board, Chavo Viejo."

"How do you know?"

"I have been here—three times before. This is a place of good people."

The breath of The Beast begins its fierce panting. Like hell-gasps. My heart begins to drum. Nearly a year has passed since I have faced the brute. Another year before that. I am out of practice. I look at my hand. The B. Then inside I say, *I can do this.* And I know I can.

These people, it turns out, they are mostly mothers. Maybe they have lost their husbands or brothers, their daughters or their sons. Now they stand fast beside The Beast, as my fellow rider says, determined to help us. As I rush from hiding to scramble on, like a warrior from a story I have heard, one such woman approaches. A heavy one with a do-not-fool-with-me look. Arms folded, she takes a firm stance when up comes a police.

"Váyase, señora," barks the poli. "Go."

"No."

He strikes her with a fist.

"Out of my way."

This rock of a woman, she says nothing but holds firm.

He strikes her again.

I can no longer stand this, hitting a woman who is trying to defend me. Like a snake I strike back. I am weak and have no weapon so, with my ragged teeth, I bite him.

"¡Cabrón!"

The poli curses and grabs for his gun.

Warrior Woman swats it away.

Eyes murderous, the poli whirls and goes after his gun—and after easier prey.

All along the tracks the story is the same. The locals standing up for us against the police.

Sometimes arrested, sometimes injured. The local people, young and old, heroes to us Beast Riders.

I look at Warrior Woman with thanks.

She presses a plastic bag of food into my hand. Softly she says, "You could be my own boy Juan. Que Dios te bendiga."

"Que Dios la bendiga," I say.

At last the train begins pulling away and I dash for it. Then, in a big confusion of scuffling and shouting, I am atop The Beast again.

Somewhere, though the train is in motion, somebody is strumming a guitar, singing "México lindo y querido," an old song Papi sang in our milpita. The voice is so sweet, so clear, my heart aches.

"—just tell them that I am sleeping, tell them to bring me back here, if I should die far from you, Mexico lovely and dear."

All along The Beast, people begin singing, even not-Mexicans. *"México lindo y querido, si muero lejos de ti . . ."* They sing a prayer, an absolute prayer.

XII

As in Serafina's village, on The Beast, every-where, I am El Chavo Viejo. My hair is not salt and pepper. Just pure and solamente sal. El Chavo Viejo. I have earned it. This name is good with me.

The moon is high this night. Moonlight pours down upon train and riders alike, a great spill of moon. I look far down the train. Moon. Moon. Moon. All riders are silvered with light. Glowing. I look down at myself. I am glowing too. I, now silver-hair, Manuel Flores.

A child near me holds on to his mother and tugs on my shirt. "I am hungry." He pleads. Maybe it is the moon glow, for in this moment I remember these same words coming from my own mouth. Before I met Señor Santos.

"Take this," I say, breaking in half a torta I have bought from a vendor.

"Gracias," he says, hungrily taking a bite.

This train is not a crowded one. So carefully I arise and move to a place where I can nearly be alone. I look up at the olden face, luminous and holy. I feel a sound lift in my throat. Like a wolf I howl at the moon. Then—somebody is howling howling beside me. Night pouring down, light pouring down, we howl, we howl.

For a time then, all is silence. Who would speak in this silvery presence?

The other wolf, he is a boy, younger than me. He wears a worn-out cap—who knows what color?—silver now. Beneath the bill his eyes spark like obsidian chips. Cejas, eyebrows, go swooping across his small brow. Silver ones.

When the moon retreats he speaks.

"Hola, lobo," says this guy, splunking down beside me. Hello, wolf.

"Hola." From all that silver I am still nearly speechless.

"Who are you?"

"Manuel Flores, El Chavo Viejo. Who are you?"

This small wolf with the cap, he pulls it off, and hair hair billows from beneath. A silver riverspill.

"I am Inés."

"Do not trust anybody," I say with urgency. Like I am an old hand at this. "Put back your cap." Girls especially are in danger on The Beast.

"I have been watching you, Chavo Viejo," says Inés, stuffing her hair beneath the cap again, "From over there I have seen you share half of nearly nothing. Besides, you are part wolf. You I can trust."

For a moment I just gape at her face.

"Here then," I say smiling, holding out to her the rest of my torta, "Take half of nearly nothing."

Inés, she is all cejas. Something from my school days comes back to me. This one, she resembles a lot the one called Frida, who painted in a very weird way. On our classroom wall, my teacher hung a calendar with Frida's odd paintings. And a photograph of her and her fantastic eyebrows. I call Inés, Cejas.

Cejas is not beautiful. But she is. With a good smile. She brings life wherever she goes. She is like a sparrow, a small brown bird with sparking eyes always hopping hopping seeking crumbs. A plucky little bird of complete mischief that steals your tortilla from your very hand if you are not watchful. A little mischief bird that for its boldness makes you smile. Like a sparrow, Cejas is small and busy and bold.

Cejas sees things I cannot see. Feels things I cannot feel. Dreams dreams beyond my dreams. She stretches me in a magical way to open my mind, my soul.

Cejas and I, two young lone ones on a train, trying to stay alive. Instantly we become comrades. A friendship of relámpago, lightning. Right off Cejas calls us Los Intensos because we feel fierce about things. A miracle! I tell myself in wonder, *I have a friend.*

My dream is to find my brother. Cejas's dream is to find her mother, in a place called Virginia of the West. There Cejas will get a job. Her first money will go to her family, she declares in her spirited way, her sparrowness.

Cejas likes photographs. She has seen one in a store window. A picture of tortillas in a basket. Tortillas of all things. But she loves it.

"One day *I* will take photographs also," she says, her dark eyes alight with the shine of her dream. For safety against bad ones, her hair is now always hidden.

Comes now her long braid of words. "Plain things—jars, petates, cactus, old fountains, old walls, old faces. Whatever I like I will snap. Maybe even sell," she adds.

At these times Cejas speaks with such grit, such fervor, such fire, I believe she might just do this.

The Beast rushes on. Cejas becomes bored.

"Now I will take photos," she says in a voice of secrets and hops up, balancing against me to not fall off.

"You are loca," I say, "and completamente reckless."

"Where is the harm in being a little reckless?"

In my mind I see death, but I do not say so.

"Come on." She beckons with her little hand. And of course, under her spell, I cannot say no.

Suddenly Cejas kneels down. Beside a mother and child, wrapped in the same torn shawl. Like us, they are tired—exhausted really—from being vigilant against assaults, from trying to stay on The Beast. They are ragged and dirty, but these things do not hide their love. *"Click."* Cejas works her pretend camera. "See?" she says, turning to me. Perched here on top of this raging beast, she captures who Beast Riders are.

Cejas clicks her camera again and again. Maybe the subject is a ladder of the train that Beast Riders grasp for their lives. Or a broken shoe abandoned—though not for long. One time she finds a huddled guy, completely filthy, gripping a filthy doll. She clicks him. Enraged, the man leaps up, yelling "¡Ladrona!" Thief! Cejas darts away from him, jumping jumping with care from car to car, crouching against the wind, shouting to me all the time, "Do not look down! Do not look down!"

At last we escape the furious man.

"Photography is dangerous," she says, not smiling.

I look at her, panting.

XIII

It is three years now since I left my home. Three years of struggle. Trickery, deception, capture, beating. These things I have known in trying to reach my goal, Toño. I am nearly fifteen, and I am one hundred. But for all of my setbacks I am strong strong.

Cejas and I are friends of the soul but going separate ways. She to Virginia of the West, me to The Angels.

"Take this," she says to me soon after we meet, her dark eyes sparking. She holds out her hand toward me.

"What?" I ask, seeing nothing.

"My camera."

"Oh, Cejas," I say, my throat tightening. "I cannot take your most treasured thing."

"Do not worry, Manuelito." Cejas shoots me a tear-bright look. "I will find another."

I reach out my hand to receive the magical camera.

When at last we take different trains, we do not say adiós, only hasta—until. For you never know when a sparrow with wide dreams and little bright eyes will come hopping hopping into your life again.

Another stretch on The Beast and then, thanks to the tips of Beast Riders who have been here before, like a miracle here I am now. In a camp beside a big river that thrashes thrashes before me, deep and murky. The Río Bravo they say. Called Rio Grande on the other side. With Cejas's enchanted camera I take a picture of this great river that I soon must cross.

The air is heavy heavy. Steamy. I am sweating like a tamal, with fear of the crossing and of the heat. As always I am called Chavo Viejo. And I am. This gray day in late January, among perfect strangers all looking across the river with yearning eyes to a glittering place for a glittering future, quietly I become older—fifteen. Nobody knows this but the river, wide wide and weary since forever with stories of others like us.

Here, surrounded by people and yet alone, I celebrate myself.

I think of the piñata song. *Dale dale dale. No pierdas el tino, porque si lo pierdes, pierdes el camino.* Ay Dios, I hope with all my hope that I do not lose the road. The Angels. That is the way.

From here I can see the United States. Gringolandia. Toño seems close now, but he is still far from me. Since my beating I have not spoken with him. Forever it seems.

For a long time, after sundown, I stand in the dark, held in the palm of night.

This place I have reached. Like The Beast it is dangerous but not as dangerous as the big city nearby. Here, at least, some of the Beast Rider brotherhood would help me if I needed it. The camp swarms with rateros and killers but mostly with ragged people like me, who have dreams so close that still may not ever be lived. Dreams once shimmering, then fading away. People who need jobs or seek family, who, to keep going these long rough years, have begged and scrounged for food. When starving, even stolen it. They have faced death from the trains. They have faced gangs. Now somehow they have to make it.

There on the other side of the river, dreams barely flicker, like the last gleaming of the day's sun.

Last chance. Last chance.

I will cross that river, I promise myself, *even though I cannot swim.* Then Abue's words come swimming back to me. *Hold on to my hand even when I have gone away from you.* And I do that, with all my might.

There comes a day I have been waiting for. The day I call Toño again. I have no cell phone, but somebody lends me one—for a price. My last pesos.

Before calling, I take my time, trying to remember my brother's voice. In my mind I try to hear it, but it is from my heart that it comes spooling. Just a plain voice. But dear. The years, the years. Since when I told him I was coming. Will he sound the same?

Then—Toño is on the line.

I wait, trembling. I cannot trust my voice. I breathe deep. And so for a time only the silence speaks.

"It is you?" I say softly at last.

"It is me."

Before our hastas, Toño promises to tell our family that I am okay. Then quickly we make a plan. Next thing, I am meeting a coyote, smuggler of people, one who will get me where I need to go. I tell Toño that I am now a white-hair so the coyote will know me. Toño will send him money when I am safe in the United States. Toño knows this one from his own dark journey. Toño knows that the coyote cannot completely be trusted—who of his kind can?—yet this dangerous man is my best chance. He is El Alacrán, The Scorpion.

Toño's last advice: Do not anger him and do what he says. He has killed people.

I wonder, *How easily would he kill me?*

By my white hair he knows me at once. Coming toward me like some crawling thing. "Chavo Viejo" is all he says.

El Alacrán. He is named for the hard-shelled old man of the desert. But he is more like a pirate walked straight from a story a teacher once read to my class. Dark-skinned, bearded, with broken teeth and a broken smile, if ever one erupts. This one, he bristles with knives and has the body of a crusher of bones. To complete the picture, El Alacrán wears an eye patch, from when the eyeball was gouged out. A pirate eye patch. De verdad. Really. Everything about him seems black black. When he talks—a rare thing—even his speech. Toño warned me to be wary, for when The Scorpion is not snarling and slashing himself out of brawls, he drinks.

¡Dios mío! This is the guy Toño has chosen to bring me closer to him. Now my life is completely in the hands of El Alacrán. Well, him and his "team" waiting on the other side. For hardly anybody crosses alone. The danger of capture is too high. The saying goes, "It takes a network to smuggle a man."

A day at still-dark dawn. El Alacrán and I steal to the edge of the big-water river. Many hopeful river-crossers are creeping close, ready to churn into the waters. But the burning gaze of El Alacrán keeps them at a distance from us. From the Glittering Side, Border Patrol guys roar, "Go back! Go back!"

No stars. Not one. But my eyes quickly grow used to the dark. Already I feel the steamy heat coming. Soon it will blaze.

The riverbank. My insides freeze when I am here. I cannot swim. But somehow I must, *I must.*

Here it is overgrown with bruja-haired trees and scraggy deep grass up to the shoulders. Though scary looking in the dark, these vegetations will hide us El Alacrán has said. From guys on both sides who want to catch us. Some of these tipos are armed with electric things to stun people. Most have guns with bullets to just snuff them lifeless. They prowl the tall grasses and the witch-haired trees waiting waiting, to stop people like me.

They are supposed to keep unarmed people alive Toño has told me. But often they do not. They just shoot. Probably they would even shoot a turtle trying for a river crossing. That is what I think.

For days before we make our move of danger—to cross over—El Alacrán, eyes glazed from guzzling Tequila, has slurred into my ear certain survival rules: "Chavo Viejo, listen good. When we go, follow me. Do not say one stinking word. Do not move one stinking weed. Do not take one stinking breath or we may be stinking dead."

"Got it?"

"Sí."

From him, "stinking" sounds like the worst word ever to pass lips.

Crack! He gives me a wicked slap that sprawls me to the ground.

"Not one stinking word," he snarls as if we have already begun our escape.

I tremble at his ferocity. I have got it. Ay do I!

This is it. The moment that I have been struggling toward these three terrible years. I feel deep danger, sí. But I feel also an excitement that I have never before known. I feel my life about to change forever.

"Now!" El Alacrán hisses. And into the mouth of peril we plunge.

We slide through the tall grasses on our panzas. Silent silent. I feel fright beyond fright. There are whirlpools, I have heard. There are snakes. But the guys with guns are scarier than snakes. Snakes do not shoot.

I think of El Alacrán's rules. I try for silence. I try for stillness. But what if the gunmen can hear my heart thundering? What if they can see my whole self shaking the grasses? Suddenly panic overtakes me. I have not told him that I cannot swim. If he knows this, he himself might just hold me under.

Abue, I pray, *hold on to my hand. Keep me from drowning in this fearsome water.*

El Alacrán knows a shallow place where we can cross. But the gun-guys know it also. They tromp it. They stalk it. They wait. From nowhere now a form appears like spreading ink. An officer close by. He spots me I think and I go stiff with fear. *No, no, no,* I moan inside like a wounded thing, *I am caught again.*

Suddenly a voice shouts, "Over there! Grab him!" Others add to the noise. They are after some other poor soul. There come frenzied rustlings. Scramblings. El Alacrán moves fast fast. Whatever plan he had before has changed.

"Run for it! Now!" he whisper-rasps.

I scream a prayer inside me and plunge for a little lump of land groping itself into the shallower waters. Squelching through the sucking mud, I make it. Thanks to Dios. No swimming. No drowning. No getting killed—not even by El Alacrán.

Shots blare behind me. Somebody wails, "¡Me mataron!" They killed me.

I just stumble, scramble, limp-run like a crazy thing alongside El Alacrán, never once looking back. My feet, heavy with my soaking tennis shoes, feel El Norte beneath them, but they do not pause.

They keep going, carrying me deep into the trees of this riverbank, deep into the land of Tejas.

The witch-haired trees and the grass and El Alacrán, they have helped. But mostly the guy who got wounded—or killed. By distracting those who guard this river crossing, he has, without knowing it, gotten me across to safety. Now the sun is full up, warm, comforting. Somewhere a dove mourns. A thought flickers in my brain. *I wish I knew that man's name.*

XV

So. Another miracle. The most miraculous so far. The Beast is behind me! The river is at my back! After plannings and more plannings by El Alacrán and the rest, dodging bands of police and border patrols, I Manuel Flores, shivering with fear and cold, have touched the earth of the United States. This ruedacaca, trying again again, has reached this place at last. Toño. Now he is closer.

I finally stop running, double over and pant pant. My sides are heaving from hobbling so fast. El Alacrán allows me half a moment to recover. My clothes are torn by the yanking claws of the trees. Because of my great fright I remember little of the river crossing except the cry of the man who saved me and my burst for freedom.

I am dripping with the big waters and mud of the Rio Grande. These run down my legs and *splop* to the ground. I close my eyes to better feel the falling water. The water I have crossed. *I have made it!* I think in wonder.

Quickly, with my pretend-camera from Cejas, I click a picture. Of my muddy shoes standing firmly upon the soil of this land. I hope that my first tennis shoes, stolen by thugs, somehow got this far. But mostly I pray that Cejas has.

What would Abue and Papi think if they saw me now? In my mind I see the hand of this America opening to me. I feel Toño near near. Through all my trials, this is the one time I allow myself tears.

"¡Muévete, güey!" El Alacrán curses at me to keep going.

We run like the devil from the Border Patrol shouting shouting. Well, El Alacrán runs, I hobble. They know we are here. In spurts we rush. We crouch behind bushes. We rush. We crouch. We rush again. My breath is gone, but I keep going. Through barbed-wire fences. Past a water tank. A

shack. Till suddenly lights blink—on, off, on, off—
ahead. My heart bangs—on, off, on, off—too when I
see the signal. The Border Patrol has caught us!

But no. The rest of the coyote-team is here in a
van, bashed around and scraped by many escapes, I
believe. I think, *This van has seen some things.* The
team is popping with impatience to get away. I look
around for El Alacrán. To say my thanks. For saving
me—and for not in an anger-burst killing me. But,
like a fistful of smoke, he is gone. Vanished. ¡Púfalas!

At once these strangers whisk me off in the van.
Shivering in my wet clothes, I am cramped in the
back on a narrow seat, next to other wet and desperate ones. Sometimes they speak of their relief in getting this far. Me, I say nothing. I just breathe breathe.

Soon we stop at a scruffy building, to bathe and
put on dry clothing. So we look like normal people, not ones escaped from a river crossing. When
we come to a checkpoint, the driver shows papers.
Also he shows money. The guy next to me pokes me
and winks. "Money is the way to grease everything,"
he says.

Then we drive a long ways. To a city. A big one.
Buildings erupt from every space of ground. And
streets. Like great gray snakes. These snake-streets

swarm with cars roaring all over the place. On the outside I set my face to be fierce. On the inside I cringe from this terrible, loud Bigness.

From the front seat somebody shoves envelopes at me and the others.

"Here's your docs," he grunts, "and dinero."

Papers and money to finish my journey. The papers are fake, I know, but the money is real.

I am tired tired. Enough to sleep for days, but I cannot. I am still tight with fear of capture and also with excitement—to be at last in the United States.

Finally, the van slows to a stop.

"Bus station. Everybody out," the driver barks.

With beautiful clean clothing and beautiful false papers, I limp toward a beautiful bus with a thin-as-a-pin dog painted on each side, a bus bound for Los Angeles, The Angels.

Nobody says adiós. Nobody says "Vaya con Dios." The van just slinks back where it came from. It is all right. Inside myself I give gracias to even the bad ones, to all those who have helped me arrive to this place. I raise my hand to nobody, and to everybody at once. I do not look back. I step into the bus.

"Hey, kid, want a seat?" somebody asks me, patting the place next to him and staring at my grandfather hair. Suspicious, I keep going.

I find a place alone, by a window, so that I can look out and watch Gringolandia rush by me. My papers, my money and food—from the coyotes, but paid for with Toño's hard-earned money—I keep on the window side of me so that nobody can just ease close and grab them. Trust nobody. The Beast Rider life. It will not be easy to let go of it. Maybe that is good.

My first bus. It is gray. It is glorious. And—it has a bathroom!

The bus hisses and coughs as we move out into traffic, but it does not jolt and lurch like The Beast. When we make turns it does not lean till you want to scream for fear of leaning right off the tracks. The wheels do not forever shriek. They keep a steady rhythm, a kind of road hum, as we roll on our way.

Looking out, I see myself in the window. Shiny. Like a mirror. I see my wild white hair—and along with it I remember the terrible things.

My plan is to stay awake. To see every mile, every inch that I pass on the way to Toño. But that plan does not happen. I think that almost at once I fall asleep on the deliciously soft seat. I must sleep nearly the whole way—a couple of days, anyway—for the next thing, the bus chuffs to a stop. I have reached The Angels.

In a small fright, I check my pockets. I have not been robbed—yet.

Once I am off, I walk slowly. I breathe carefully. In case I am moving inside of a dream. In case this moment, like a trail of cloud, floats away. Just goes. Though I barely move, my eyes flick everywhere. They search every face. Doubt grabs hold of me and will not let go. What if I got the date wrong? What if I miss him? What if—? What if—? What if—?

All sounds go still. I am no longer breathing. I am looking from some place outside. Caught in this strange silence. The world seems to slow down, to slant, and me with it. I feel suddenly stunned with emotion, stronger than I have ever known. Then, here in this bus station, standing still as stone among the many people pushing, jostling in slow and silent motion, is a person I know in my deep heart, without a signal, without a word, without a photo. Toño.

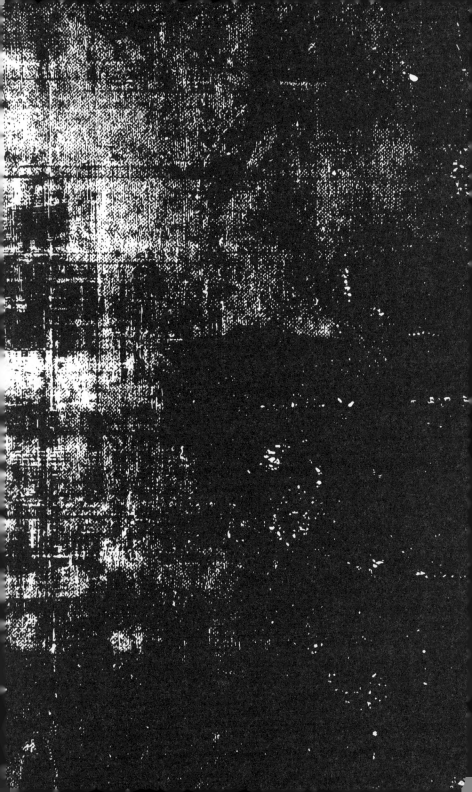

THE ANGELS

XVI

When he spots me a glow lights his face. We rush for each other and embrace, and for a long time we stay like this, holding each other. We are both shaking.

Then we just stand there amazed that this moment has come. At least I am. Toño looks amazed also.

"Dios mío, how you have grown, hermanito!" he chokes out at last. Me, I cannot speak.

I am fifteen. Almost a man. But linking my arm in his I will not let Toño go. Not for one single moment.

Nor he me, it seems, though he is older by seven years. Suddenly my feet become stupid. If on their own they would wander all over this big L.A. without a plan other than to avoid polis. But luckily Toño has one. First thing, he swerves me into a church. When the big doors creak closed we no longer hear the noise of the street.

We hear peace. For inside it is quiet, except for the rustling clothing of a few old women down on their creaky old knees. In this place there is a fragrance of incense and the whispers of all the faithful who have ever entered. There is the coolness of the much-trodden stone floors and of the waxy breath of candles. We two slip one coin each into a little box and light candles of our own. Actually, I get two candles. One for the unknown man at the river crossing. Toño and I do not speak, but I am certain we both light our velas for Mami. And we give thanks for those dear and far away and for the great miracle which has brought us to each other once again.

We kneel. Then we slide into a shaky pew. Lapped by the prayers of years, we sit in silence. In this moment I am overwhelmed by all that has befallen me—and him. And the grace that has reunited us.

Toño is grateful also, I know, for on this slab of ancient wood, in this old and holy place, shoulders touching, I can feel my brother weeping.

El Pueblo de Nuestra Señora la Reina de los Ángeles de Porciúncula. The Town of Our Lady Queen of the Angels of Porciuncula. A mouthful. This, Toño tells me, is the complete and real true name of the place where I am. Where we are, Toño and I. Together.

"Is not that the most beautiful name you have heard in your life?" he asks me vigorously.

"Sí, it is a name of glory," I say. The City of Angels. Angels brought me here, I believe.

The Angels. What a place it is. Toño and I leave the church and hurry hurry along the street, eager to call home. I look up. There are buildings tall tall with mirror sides that gleam with sun. Buildings so high they scratch the sky. They touch the clouds themselves. I feel small. Dazed. For a few heartbeats

I believe my mouth falls open. Enough for grillos to hop in, if grillos live here. Ay!

I do not for a minute forget that I have sneaked into this country. Like a wild creature, eyes darting darting, I keep checking for trouble. As I did upon my long journey to get here.

Strange trees line the streets. Their thin bare trunks reach up up up into the sky so that I must lean back to see them completely. They are topped with shaggy clumps of great big leaves that look like they might just bend these trees over at any minute. When I see them I gape, up up up.

"Palms," Toño says with a grin. "A real L.A. thing."

"Oh," I say, still gaping.

And all around us blare signs I cannot read. And impossible noise so that we hardly hear each other speak. Cars rushing rushing. Buses snorting out smoke. Motorcycles flaring past. Each time one passes, it is like the roar of The Beast. I cannot help it, I flinch.

In these first Los Angeles moments, fear trembles me. I know I will never be free of The Beast behind me. Or of somebody trying to send me back. But maybe The Angels is a different kind of beast—one that just dazes you to death.

"So, little brother," says Toño with pride in his voice, "what do you think?"

I cannot think. Truly, I cannot speak.

When we reach where Toño lives the sky-scratchers are gone. Now it is all small houses looking tired and old. Many have roofs of tejas, some already slid off to the ground, leaving gaps. Like teeth gone. These old roofs make me feel the pull of Señor Santos and his tejas, but more the tug of home. Our little adobe. My family. These houses, they are huddled together, so many, so close they are nearly crushing each other. Like the riders of The Beast.

Toño's is a tiny place in back of one of the squashed-together houses. A bougainvillea bursting with purple blooms climbs up one side of the house, as if holding it up. A bougainvillea, like of our family's home.

"Wow!" is all I can say. For this is much larger than our little adobe.

"Pretty big, huh," he answers.

His rented house has one room where he eats and sleeps, one kitchen, and—unbelievable—one bathroom *inside*. I know I will sleep well in Toño's home, my brother here with me, a roof of tejas over my head.

My brother, he is not as big as I remember. Like a plant of maíz stretching for the sun, I am taller. But he is still as full of fire as ever. Everything Toño does is urgent, with excitement, as he shows me this place. We must squeeze in many years we have lost. We must squeeze in also the places which are his Los Angeles.

As we walk into his home, comes a solemn moment. With both hands Toño touches my face and looks at me with caring.

"How are you?" he asks.

"I am alive."

We do not dwell upon The Beast. Too well we both know that story. Once I notice him flicker a look at the palm of my hand. He says nothing, but his eyes go dark. And of my white cloud of hair, the same. He does not blink. He knows how I earned it.

Right away, on Toño's cell phone, we call our family—together. At the other end the sound is like a great exhaling of worry. At once from Papi, from Abue, from our little brother and sister comes a soft "Gracias a Dios." Then for a time, from all of us, a small silence—of gratefulness. And then a pure craziness of joyful noise.

XVII

Toño wants to teach me all there is about the United States in one gulp, fast fast. His mustache jumps up and down like a being of its own, as he explains to me Los Angeles things.

The next day we visit a fish market and buy—something. Toño lifts the thing high and, grinning gleefully, slops it in my direction saying, "Here is dinner, little brother." Even when he is teasing me, I feel the sound of our home language enfold us like a mother's warm arms.

With fright I look at this mystery Toño holds. Can this be a sign of some kind? Who would believe that God made such a creature? (Who would believe He made the animals who branded me?)

"¡Ay Dios!" I shout and jump back, nearly falling to the ground. "I cannot eat that!" The words just spurt themselves out. "What is it?"

"A pulpo. Oc-to-pus."

Some limp and dangling things look like slices of our bath mat.

"I cannot eat a bath-mat animal," I insist.

"You will love it, little brother," says Toño. "I have learned to cook this dish from my girlfriend."

Girlfriend! First an oc-to-pus, then a novia. Which is worse?

I am not convinced that Cejas would want this being on her magical camera, but I decide finally that she would be delighted. *Click.* The creepy creature is forever captured.

On the way back from the fish place, near Toño's home I see a viejito, an old man, on the porch of a tiny house, sitting in a wooden chair. He is taking in the scene, I think, but without seeming to.

"Who is that?" I ask warily, but not pointing.

"A neighbor. A Japan man. He lives alone. I do not know him."

Toño does not know him. I gape. "How can you not know your neighbor?"

"This is Los Angeles."

Poor guy, I think. *He might wait forever for somebody to talk to him.*

I look in the man's direction. In a not-staring way, he looks at me. Suddenly I shudder. My mind swings from *Poor guy* to *What if he is a bad one? What if he turns us in?*

At home Toño rinses our mysterious meal, grinning grinning with wicked glee all the while.

Maybe I laugh at this thing that at first gave me a big fright. If I laugh I do not recognize that good sound. It has been a long time. . . .

"Look here, little brother," Toño says. "These are ten-ta-cles." He stretches the word out, holding up each one as he does. "Now you say 'ten-ta-cle.'"

"Ten-ta-*quel.*"

"Now," like a stiff school teacher Toño says, "we count."

I wait.

"Hold up a tentacle and say 'one.' One is the same as 'uno.'"

I do not wish to touch the bath-mat animal, but I get used to it. This octopus is so ugly, it is a bit simpático. From one, on we go, for two, three, and the rest. These tentacles they are rubbery and sometimes slip out of my hand.

"So how many tentacles?" asks Toño.

"¿Diez?" I mumble, because I lost count.

"Eight," says my teacher in disgust. "Again."

Tentacle by tentacle, in this way I begin to learn English.

XVIII

I do not slide into this new life easily. All things are different from my pueblito. Los Angeles is crazy with noise. And people and cars racing all over the place. At home some people still ride horses and donkeys.

Toño is a magnificent teacher and brother. "Magnificent" is one of my English words and I am proud of it. The trouble is that he is usually not with me. Nights, he works cleaning office-building bathrooms. Days, he sleeps like a big possum. Me, I am a day guy.

Always when I get up, though he is like a stone with sleeping, he has left a Post-it on the floor. A Post-it in a place so I have to step over it and cannot miss it. On this sticky little scrap is written carefully my word-of-the-day, which I must keep in my memory and use whenever the chance pops itself up.

Toño chooses these words by opening a little book he got from an English class. He took lessons to learn this language. He starts just any place, closing his eyes and letting his finger run down the page till it stops wherever it feels like it. As if his finger is choosing! This is how Toño is.

So far some of the words are: "hover," "flamboyant," "swoop," "rind," "trophy," "yikes," "stupendous," "cheese," "wyvern." "Wyvern." "Yikes" is right. A wyvern is a long-ago made-up creature with wings that is like a two-legged dragon. Just where I will use these strange words I cannot think. Maybe at McDonald's I could order a wyvern with special sauce on a sesame-seed bun.

"Toño," I say, "make your finger choose me some normal words. With yours nobody will understand me."

"Maybe not, little brother," says Toño, his eyes sparking like crazy, his Pancho Villa mustache in vigorous motion, "but you will have a fantastical vocabulario."

True. And, apart from other ways, I know from this game of words that my brother loves me.

Like I said, I am a day guy. Toño is nocturnal (word-of-the-day). Only on weekends we do things together, along with his octopus-cooking girl-friend. Even though she is from Durango, this novia is named Sinaloa, for another Mexico state. In a big originality, her parents chose it, she says, for the beautiful sound. I believe they are right. Sinaloa. Beautiful. Like falling water.

These two, they are not married, so Sinaloa has her own place. Through our home she comes and goes, a crisp and sparkling breeze.

Like my friend Cejas from The Beast, this one she has a good smile. One that is open and true, not meaning some other thing. When she smiles at Toño, it is very warm, very loving. When she smiles at me—once she knows me—it is loving but in a different way.

Whenever I am with Sinaloa I think of Cejas. I wonder how her dream is going.

I first know that Sinaloa likes me when she helps me with the dishes. I wash. She dries. Toño, in a big clatter, he puts stuff away. It is a weekend so he is not working. I say nothing, but the hot water hurts my hand. After all this time the scar is still tender.

While we work, Sinaloa teases me a little, but with good humor.

"What crazy hair you have, Manuelito. It is like it has its own all-over-the-place life."

"Yep," I say. "It grows however it feels."

We laugh about my hair's wildness. But she never mentions the whiteness.

One day, like my Señor Santos, Sinaloa attacks my hair with scissors. Me in my complete clothes, in the bathtub. "So your pelo loco, like clippings of grass, will not disarrange this house," she says. She talks in a sparkling way, and fast, while the scissors *chomp chomp*, and I worry she may be chopping chopping big holes where there should not be any. But when she does her inspection of this work, she flares her honest smile again. She pats my face. "Qué guapo," she says. How handsome.

Another good thing about Sinaloa, she can cook things apart from octopus. Things of my home. My favorite is just plain guacamole which even I can make and which goes like this:

Into a bowl scoop some avocados from their skins. Have ready chopped-up tomatoes, onions, serrano chiles—not in exceso—and sí, an *exceso* of cilantro. (The cilantro leaves, I pick from the stems with my fingers. Sometimes I crush a leaf and hold it to my nose. ¡Qué rico! How delicious is the smell! Squash the avocados, then toss in the rest. Salt and a little lime juice come last. Then mix mix, but not too much. And there you have your guacamole. (Unless you eat it in one fast craziness, you can put in avocado seeds, so it does not go brown.)

At home, when we had the money, we made tacos of guacamole and little fried red grasshoppers. (Not the big ones whose legs get stuck in your teeth.) Very crunchy. Very tasty. These grasshoppers do not seem to live in The Angels. ¡Qué lástima! What a pity!

When I prepare this guacamole with Sinaloa, the smell of the warm tortillas for tacos rises, perfuming the kitchen. Then real as anything I can name, Abue ghosts into the room. *Hold on to my hand. . . .* In my heart I do, and I yearn myself home.

Each meal, before I eat these beautiful foods, I remember times of hunger on The Beast journey. As I look at my plate full full—or even at one lone taco—I think of my own luck and of those still struggling, or dead. Like Papi over the simple things of life, I bow my head.

Those two, Toño and Sinaloa, think I should go back to school since here I do not work a milpita. School. A dream. But over me always hovers a gloom, that I will be noticed one day—from my hand maybe—and sent to Mexico again. Fear is always a little bit crawling down my back.

One Saturday I overhear Toño and Sinaloa talking about going to the movies, a big splurge, so I jump right in and all in a rush I say, "What will we see? ¿Vaqueros? Can we have palomitas?" I think I would love to see a movie, a cowboy one. A sometimes treat, already I love popcorn.

A glance slides between them so quick, if I were not looking right at them it would have skimmed by. I realize they are planning to go just the two of them. Stupid me. So I catch myself and say, "Well, after all, maybe not. I am tired."

"Sure?"

"Yep. You watch for me."

"Okay," Toño easily agrees. "We will bring you popcorn."

"And a Coke," Sinaloa chimes in.

Next morning, when I get up, a small paper tub is waiting for me. And a watery Coke. The buttery fumes still rising from the tub, I think that is what pulls me from bed. Here in the United States this treat is called "popcorn." "Popcorn" is fine, but I call it by its Mexico name which is more beautiful: "palomitas." Little doves. I eat the palomitas for breakfast. Even cold they taste good. But for some reason they make me feel lonely.

Day in January. The tail end of the month. A year after my river crossing. At dawn parrots pour into the sky as if an unseen hand is opening, letting go a glittering gleam of green. Where do they come from? Who knows? But daily they stream over us, brightly, greenly, noisily, like squawking leaves. These birds are a big gift to the gray skies of Los Angeles.

On the floor, in a place I cannot miss, a Post-it awaits me. Groan. The word-of-the-day—

"Fiesta"!

Somebody has been watching, for at once come gigglings. Rustlings. Shufflings. Then songs bloom. "Las mañanitas" . . . and "Happy Birthday to You"!

Yelling "Happy sixteen years!" Sinaloa and Toño burst forth bulging with piñatas piñatas, one for each of my lost birthdays since Toño left I guess. These piñatas, they are all little donkeys. Blue.

Toño. In this great splash of love, he has remembered my dearest childhood wish.

We—and the piñatas—attempt a rustling embrace. Inside I feel swollen like an absolute full moon. The tears of this boy, tears held back these many years, come falling.

By greatest grace, here I am in The Angels holding close close this dear piece of family whom I thought I had lost.

XXI

Trauma del tren, train trauma, that is what Toño
says that I have, over these long months with
him. Train trauma. Upness, downness, sadness, madness, all-over-the-placeness. These feel-
ings are ever there, like a rat gnawing at the edges of
my spirit.

Sometimes I stare at the B on my hand and I
cannot believe how I got it. B. Believe. And then I
do. I remember all over again. I do not go out much,
my mind wanders to ugly events, I sag around, not
able to make decisions and I feel tired tired.

I need to get myself out of this. I need a real job,
not just work around the house. To help Toño with

small costs, mostly food and to make telephone calls to our family. Also to repay some of his heavy coyote money. I find out he had to borrow a lot. Though he says I do not, I owe him that. With the rent I cannot help.

Like teaching me English, Toño gets me ready for job searching. Because my papers are false, I cannot show them to just anybody. That could get me sent back to my pueblito in a finger snap. Instead, in a knot of nerves, I must go to a certain street corner and wait. For this kind of work I need no papers.

Toño tells me what to do. "Stand in front," he urges, "so you will be seen. Wear a big sombrero, so you will *really* be seen. Most important, look smart."

So I practice a couple of smart faces.

Toño says, "You look crazy."

When I am on the street corner I plan to go for "look awake."

At first I join other people from other places who do not have the right papers for real work either. They work in spurts, whenever they can. A small job here, a smaller job there. But not full-on steady-money work. In the gloom of dawn they appear like fantasmas, phantoms, and wait—in parking lots, on street corners—looking their best, hoping for work from people who drive by. They will mow lawns, weed gardens, wash cars, windows. Anything. They are patient, this band of phantoms. Even when some people shout things at them like *Job-stealers! Animals! Criminals! Scum! Go back where you came from!*

These shouters scare me to the bone, they seem so much like the polis and Border Patrol—those bad ones who tried to stop me. Maybe truly they fear for their jobs, but mostly, I believe, they simply do not like foreigners.

Sometimes the polis plunge in and arrest the job-hunters they can catch, to send them home. Then I do not return for many days, my fear of them is so strong.

We hopefuls, we talk a little with each other, but mostly we do not, so eager are we to spot a job-giver and get work.

When I am among the others hoping and waiting, I imagine I can hear each pleading voice, loud as a chorus: *Give me a chance. Give me a chance. Por Dios.*

>>>>>>>>>>

One morning ripe with sun a lady drives up to the place where we hopeful workers are waiting. It is illegal for her to hire any of us, but still she is here. She knows she can hire us for cheap. Her car is big and shiny. A one called SUV. She rolls down one window and snaps. "Who can do gardening for me?"

"I can!" I shout above the others, shooting her my most extremely awake look. "No problema. I am experienced." I am experienced with maíz. Gardening. How hard can it be?

Toño's tips pay off. I have the magic word "experienced." I stand near the front, with my wide sombrero. Of course, it does not hurt that I am tall. For this job the lady chooses me and a guy about my same age named Lorenzo. As I walk to the car she jabs the air, toward my leg. She has noticed my limp! My heart drops. "No problema," I say in a big confident way and keep going. So she orders, "Well, get in."

We jumble into her car and go to her house. The whole way she says not one word. Then a word-river floods out from her which I struggle to under-stand. My words-of-the-day—like "stupendous" and "wyvern," the dragon—are of no help. This work, it seems not to be about dirt and flowers at all. It is chopping down—with machetes—a tree of huge tallness. An eucalipto. A monstruo. "Stupendous" I can use after all.

I hate to kill a tree, especially one as grand as this that has taken many years to reach this size. But I want to help Toño with expenses. The lady and us, we settle upon a price. It is cheap, but what can Lorenzo and I do? We need the work, so we are stuck. The tree lady knows this. I bet there is a big smirk down somewhere in place of her heart.

By this time my fears are many. Fear of trains. Fear of robbers. Fear of starvation. Fear of drowning. Fear of polis. To this list I now add fear of eucaliptos.

This monster looms close to the casa, very close.

"Have you done this before?" I ask Lorenzo hopefully, and in Spanish, when the lady goes inside for the machetes.

"Never," he says.

This eucalipto, it is like a hell-test. I do not know what I am doing. Neither does my compañero. Easily we could fail. And fall. But what if we have success? What if we get lucky and actually topple this thing? What if then it flattens the house?

The lady returns and keeps talking at us, louder and louder as if that will help us understand better, about extreme carefulness. About her precious house. About how if we go wrong she will call the police. Lorenzo understands her mean words. I understand her mean voice. My nerves are needles. But I cannot back down. I need the money.

Looking up at el monstruo makes me dizzy dizzy. Shinnying up is worse. I bind myself to the tree with a nearly falling-to-pieces rope. Holding tight to my machete, with strongest urgings, I talk myself to the top.

"Are you scared?" Lorenzo asks once he is also up.

"Aterrado." I believe my smile is the weakest one ever tried in the history of people.

Then one by one Lorenzo and I hack branches off till the tree is pretty pelón. Like a pole. For fear of falling, we do not talk much, except I learn that Lorenzo is from Honduras. Far from home like me. And lonely. His voice tells me this last thing.

Here we are, two guys from far places, whacking at a tree we hold nothing against, for a hard lady who cares for nobody but her own face-stretched self, about to plunge to our deaths. Suddenly we both spurt forth with laughs—petrified ones. *What am I doing,* I wonder, *up in this sky-scratcher tree, in this loco Los Angeles, when I could be safe in our milpita, shawled with blessed dust, pushing a plow behind Trini?*

Being with deep dizziness, I pray that I do not chop myself with my machete, or fall and break my neck. Between Lorenzo and me this work takes some days, in which we are sweating and covered in wood chips and leaves, grazed by falling limbs and always overcome and reeking reeking with the eucalipto smell like medicine. It is itchy work. My worry is constant. What if our ancient ropes do not hold? We are up here like eagles with no aeries (word-of-the-day)—and no wings.

How could I have survived the Beast journey, the gangs, the polis, the big-river crossing, only to die by tree?

While doing this labor I remember the words of Señor Santos. *Your work—in even the smallest things—it is a mirror of you.* So, though I feel miserable, I labor well for this misery of a person.

As if it is not hard enough, the lady of the tree is so stingy she does not offer food, she does not offer water. But often, far below, like a nasty little dog, she barks cautions and orders. I just keep saying to her "No problema," and I keep hacking.

When the big limbs are gone we shinny back down and set our machetes to biting into the trunk. *Thwack! Thwack! Thwack!* My arms become aching from this tough work. Chopping an eucalipto is like chopping brick. And then comes the time that it begins to make a funny noise and to tremble. ¡Ay Jesús! We have no control over el monstruo. It has chosen to topple. To topple in all its big heaviness for the casa! The house will be squashed and I will be caught by polis. The lady screams. Lorenzo and I pray. As el monstruo falls I feel a wind, as if the thing is letting out all of its breath. Then—a miracle!—in a great rustle and crash it comes down—missing the casa by one pulgada.

Though we successfully miss her house by an inch, the lady is in full fury. Enraged completely.

"Fools! You are useless!" Lorenzo translates quickly. "You can't speak English. You can't do anything! You Mexicans are all alike!" She screams this, even though Lorenzo is from Honduras. "I will not pay you a penny! Go! You are a disease infecting our country! We need walls against you!" She slams the gate and locks us out. "And you call yourselves gardeners!" She shrieks one last insult.

I never called myself anything but desperate.

I am a young man with one bad eye, who hobbles, who has left his family, who has lost a tooth and been broken by bandits to reach this place to find honest work. Walls against me? She needs my work. She needs to let me in. My heart plunges like a crazy thing. That one, she is certain to call the police, so Lorenzo and I, we just get out of there.

"¡Suerte!" Lorenzo calls to me on the run when we part ways. Good luck!

"¡Igual!" Same for you!

I have lost a week of my life. I have lost my pay. Also I have lost some faith. There are good people in The Angels I am certain, but that lady, she is not one.

Somewhere near, in this craziness that is The Angels, I hear a siren. I believe I see police-car lights pulsing, so I hobble myself along as fast as I can. At night when I finally find my way home, I dream. Angry voices shout at me *Job-stealer! Criminal! Go back where you came from!*

Job-stealer? The truth is nobody else would take such job. Nobody would chop down an eucalipto a machetazos but a desperate guy like me.

Why do they spit out such names?

Do they not know that I am a person like them?

Do they not see my face?

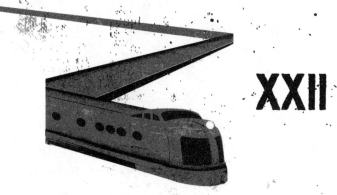

XXII

Time passes. Time and time. One year. Another. Moving slowly like creaking cart wheels. I work. Toño works. When I do not have work I do jobs around the house. Cleaning, washing windows, cooking also. Like that. We do not have a vacuum cleaner, so I sweep a lot. I always take longer than I need to, for the sound of the broom is a comfort, whispering whispering like Abue's broom at home.

Once, ants seeking water and crumbs enter during a time of drought. I know what it is to be hungry and thirsty, so I do not want to kill them. I do not want to kill anything. Still we cannot live with swarms of ants, so with poison spray I "do them in." That is an American way to say it.

When the bodies are dry I sweep them into a little heap—like coffee grounds—then put them in the trash. I spend some time then scrubbing the floor where the invasion took place, getting rid of the smell of poison.

While I am doing these chores, my mind floats. Toño and Sinaloa, they may love me, but they are one. I am an outsider, really. I begin to feel uneasy about other things too. I wonder, *Waiting in the street for a job to come. Killing ants. Chopping random trees. Is this all there is for me?*

I am alive, but not. Just breathing does not count as living.

"Look for signs," Abue tells me still when we talk quickly on the phone and I ask where my life will go. "Follow them."

The old man who is Toño's neighbor but not neighbor. I see him whenever I pass his house to go home. At first I pretend not to see him. The safe path. But now we recognize each other. We do not speak but our eyes meet. Two lonely guys, I guess, living on the same street.

I decide not to wait for La Vida to carry me like a leaf on a stream. I think about things that I like to do, my mind rambling over my years. The big one is to shape tejas. In the olden way, as I did with Papi and with Señor Santos. Making a thing with your hands is good. In the work you leave some of your self.

With me tejas become a Thing. I ask Toño if he knows anybody who makes them. No, he does not. But he asks around, knowing that I am excited about this. Word goes out. Toño asks somebody. Somebody asks somebody else. This way is what gringos call "the grapevine." And it works. One time before Toño falls into bed after his all-night work, he leaves me a Post-it. Not one word, but a tejas-place name. Somebody along his grapevine has recommended me, so I had better brincar, jump over there, and grab a job while I can. (This information fits on two Post-its actually.)

That is what I do. Brinco. I jump for this job. In The Angels this means I must take a bus, walk, take another bus, walk, and so on. All this costs. Time and money. And then maybe you will come upon the place you are looking for, if you do not get lost.

Mission Tiles is the name of the place. A mission is like a big church, so the name sounds good to me. I do not call first. I just go, thinking it is better to present myself, looking ready to jump into the work.

Mission Tiles is the furthest thing from Señor Santos's small tile makings that I can imagine. It is a factory. Huge. Like a barn. But not with soft whinny-ings of horses or lowings of cows. Not with a rooster or a cat to press its track into a soft tile piece. To say *I was here*. None of that. Knees to bend the pieces are not involved either. It is all clangings and bangings as tiles are spat out by big machineries onto what is called a conveyor belt.

This place also has the endless yelling of the foreman. He is called Half, nobody knows why. Another worker tells me that Half says he was once a marine and that he is proud to talk like one. That is, yell like one, in a constant ugliness stream. If this one is Half, I do not want the whole.

When I am working here, I think of Señor San-tos, who probably never used a curse word, not even exclaimed "¡Ay Chihuahua!" I would not be proud of such a thing. Neither would a truly good marine.

All day long, workers, me also, snatch tiles one at a time from the belt. We smooth the edges, then put the tiles back. Always working fast. In here it is hot hot. Red tile dust covers everything, everybody. (I like this part. It reminds me of the blessing of the tile dust of Señor Santos, and the blessing of the dust of our milpita.) The finished pieces are baked and stacked. By machines. If we work too slowly—or drop a tile by accident—Half curses us and makes us pay for the broken one. Sometimes he just barges up to somebody and swats a tile from his hand, shattering it on purpose. "Clumsy idiot! A dollar for that!" He grins, grabs the money and stuffs it into his pocket. A dollar the worker needs.

These workers they are like me. No papers. At least not real ones. So Half bullies us and gets away with it. We can do nothing, except leave. And we cannot afford that.

When I am home and it is quiet I think of my family. I think of what they have taught me my whole life. Never quit a work. Be humble, be proud of your labor, finish. But this work it is different. There is no finish. There is nothing to be proud of working in this tejas place. I am humble, but machine tejas are not my path. My choices are few but still I have them. In this life there is something for me that is not a cold teja machine and a colder-still bully. I quit.

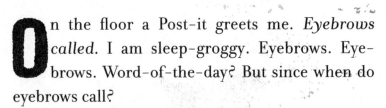

XXIII

On the floor a Post-it greets me. *Eyebrows called.* I am sleep-groggy. Eyebrows. Eyebrows. Word-of-the-day? But since when do eyebrows call?

"Eyebrows!" I suddenly hoot out loud. Cejas! I remember that before she left I gave her Toño's number. I look at the ceiling as though there is a full moon up there, and I let loose a long wolf howl.

That one, of course she has a cell phone.

I am awake when Toño comes home.

"You got her number?" I ask first thing, without even a greeting for him.

"Whose?"

"Eyebrows's! In Virginia of the West!" I say it as if any fool would know this.

"Eyebrows do not have numbers," Toño teases.

"Come on, man, give it over."

Toño makes a big show of trying to find it till finally I tackle him and start invading his pockets myself.

"Hands off." We giggle like little boys.

"Tell me about Eyebrows," he says, squirming from me.

"Eyebrows, brother. You wear them on your face," I say, digging with my fingers to find the best tickles.

"Enough!" He begs, limp with laughs. Then with fake surprise he holds up a bit of paper and says, "Well now, what is *this?*"

I do not snatch the paper, for fear of tearing the number. I wait. Like a dog with a steak dangling just out of its reach.

"Ton-*yo!*" I plead, "We must call!"

"Now?" asks my brother, stretching out my frustration, knowing I am in his clutches. "What time is it in West Virginia?"

I do not care what time it is. I care about talking with Cejas. But I now slow down, going for nonchalance. "It is not midnight, if that is what you mean. I think it is a good calling time."

"Who is this Eyebrows you have so carefully hidden from me?" Toño asks in a needling way. *Ay!* I think. *Teasing is coming for the rest of my life.*

"Toño, let me call her or I will keep you awake all day!" I shout. My nonchalance is vanished.

"Here 'mano. Enjoy your call." He hands me his phone.

I close the door and start dialing. My hands are shaking. How funny. She is just a girl.

The cell seems to ring forever. Finally, somebody answers. A miracle! Cejas.

"Hola," I say, feeling all of a sudden shy. "It is me."

"Wolf boy?"

Then comes a small silence and Cejas says, "You are smiling, right?"

"Yep." I feel my face splitting into two pieces with a grin.

Cejas jumps right in, telling me in runaway words how her life has been. "My mami is fine and she loves me and so do her new children which she had over here in Virginia and one is called Virginia for that reason and one is called West because that is the rest of this state's name and Mami likes the joke of it and I am not hungry every day anymore and I work for a photographer, the old-timey kind with an old-timey camera that stands on stick legs and is heavier than I am and he droops a black cloth over himself like he is hiding and squeezes a bulb to take pictures of little kids and old people and all in-between ones and I get to run errands and give dulces to the little ones and I give sweets to myself also because my boss says it is okay and I hold up toys one is a bright red bird and I say "Watch the birdie" like old-timey photographers used to say and they do not watch the birdie but they do watch me because I make faces that make them happy and I believe that soon I will be snapping photos from beneath that big black cloth. . . ."

Cejas's story gallops on and on, and I feel her sparkle zing right through the phone and into my hand.

We make a plan to talk again.

"Then you can tell me *your* story," she says.

"Ha! I will be surprised to squeeze any words in," I say back. My voice is still smiling.

When the call ends I feel absolutely wrung out like laundry. That is the Cejas Effect for you.

XXIV

Toño and I, we see each other when we can. He teases me with a "How is your *girlfriend?*" when he can. Also, when we are together we call home. One worry for me is that, so far away, the dear voices will grow weaker weaker. Just fade like clouds thinned in wind. But no. When I close my eyes, the voices, the faces, they grow strong. Especially Abue's.

Aside from Toño and Sinaloa and a few calls to Cejas, I keep to myself. Here in this Los Angeles, impossibly enormous place, I am an island. Loneliness wraps me like a dark sarape, but I spill my heart to nobody.

Toño's neighbor, the Japan man, is a withered-up one with about one hundred years on him, I believe. A white-hair, as I call him. Like me. Whenever I see him he is always sitting alone in his chair on his tiny porch. I have never seen him with a visitor, not even a neighbor. Deciding that he is not a spy as I first thought, I begin to nod when I go by. At least I think I do. A little dip of the head. The Japan man, he does the same. A nod. A bow really.

He bows to *me*, Beast Rider alone, swallowed by L.A.! I cannot ignore a bow. Among many things, Abue and Papi have taught me courtesy. Next time I pass, I Manuel Flores, truster of nobody, most of all not strangers, I lift my hand in the littlest wave, like a tiny small flag. This man, he waves back, and again he bows.

Soon I am stopping—at first a little, then longer and longer—to visit the man who I learn is Mr. James Ito and who I come to think of as "my viejito." He bows. I bow. Respect we now show always upon meeting.

He is full of years and wrinkles and also full of solemnness. Yet there is something else about this old one, so bone thin but wire-tough. Always a bit ceremonious, he is the kind of person who causes you to use his full complete name.

Mr. James Ito, sí a most solemn one. At first speaking but little. But then he talks more, a slow river flowing itself along. Pretty soon I make a decision. When I am not working I will tell stories about my family and my home to this old one, to keep him from feeling alone.

Life is a twist. My plan to share stories with Mr. James Ito turns itself inside out. My stories fade away, for he begins telling stories to me. Of when he was young. Of his still-alive dreams. "We always need dreams," he says. These visits soften my own loneliness.

My viejito tells of walking in the beautiful mountains of Oregon. He tells of gardens in a way that I know he loves the earth. Then I drift off, thinking of our milpita far away. And of my family. Once Mr. James Ito tells a story in which our lives cross, though he does not know it. He says that long ago, in his green years, he and his friends were in a car, rattling along fast fast when in the distance came the long mourn of a train. At this, I stiffen.

"We were teenagers and crazy from drinking," says my viejito, "and just crazy from being young."

I am stunned that such a one would drink spirits, but I keep this thought inside myself.

The tracks were right ahead. "Faster! Floor it! We can beat it!" The train was racing. The car was racing. Then with great suddenness—two friends were dead.

"I have a scar," Mr. James Ito tells me in full solemnity. "It is long and white," he explains, "cross-hatched where long ago stitches stabbed in. Like railroad tracks." I would like to see it, but do not ask. He does not offer to show it either, being very full of dignity. Like a teller of fortunes he then gazes into my eyes darkly. "Avoid trains, young Manuel," says Mr. James Ito, speaking about his experience. But of course it is too late for that.

We are both scarred by trains.

This same night I am awakened by a shout. Mine. I am panting, wet with sweat and trembling like a moth. Shards of broken-bottle glass tumble down down in slow motion through the vision I have had. One shard is etched with a machete blade. Another with a brand, a horned B. Some with the vicious faces of bandits. And polis. Toño is not home yet. For a long time I quake in the dark.

r. James Ito. His face is a secret, hiding many things, I believe. But his is a heart that hides nothing. I do not always understand what he is saying, but I feel safe with him. Nearly from the beginning—a great wonder—I trust him. And so, soon soon, I Manuel Flores who tells nobody anything, find myself sitting beside him on a small wooden chair sipping tea from tiny cups with no handles and revealing to him the complete story of my Beast journey.

Like tears held in for a very long time, out the words come. Pouring pouring. Mine is an ugly tale, apart from the few saints who float in and out—Gabriel, Señor Santos, Warrior Woman of the train station, Serafina, the doctor, the villagers and the children, and, of course, jewel-eyed, dream-lit Cejas, friend of friends.

When at last the flow of my words slows and thins, when I have recounted the final chapter, silence comes. Too respectful to stare I believe, my viejito glances at my hair. He says only, "So. That explains it."

Then Mr. James Ito lets the silence work. I turn over in my mind these things I have been saying. And I realize in this moment how much goodness has been woven into my story. I think that from now on I will try to forget the bad. Papi would say that, like the maíz, good reaches for light. I decide. I also will reach for light.

Into the afternoon we sit side by side on two small chairs on his tiny porch, tiny teacups long empty. Mr. James Ito and I, each drifting along on his own thoughts. Two white-hairs together, remembering.

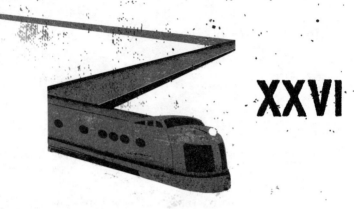

XXVI

"May I take your picture?" I ask Mr. James Ito one day. "My friend Cejas of the train gave me this camera."

At first Mr. James Ito looks puzzled by this request, seeing nothing in my hands. Then, as I move toward him he sees that the camera is imaginary and gives one of his rare and shallow smiles.

"By all means," he says with a slight bow and poses like an old-fashioned gentleman, stiff and somber but with a twinkle hiding somewhere close.

I bow also to begin.

I show him the result.

"A good likeness," says Mr. James Ito in a satisfied way.

Mr. James Ito lives in a tiny house. Much tinier than ours. It is a long time before he invites me in. Maybe, like me, he is also not a truster.

When Mr. James Ito first asks me to enter, I feel that there is something more happening than just white-haired me going into a house. That he has made a big decision, to be my friend, look out for me.

Abue taught me that people are sent to you, "guides" she calls them, to cross your path and to help you through life. There are bad ones also who try to drag you to hell-places, but you do not follow them. Like Papi's maíz you go for the light. Maybe Mr. James Ito has come to guide me in place of Abue and Papi. With his many years like the rings of a tree, his many wrinkles, his life crosses mine to give his many wisdoms. He is a sage. (Word-of-the-day.)

As we go into the house our eyes meet. We know our new situation.

I notice that Mr. James Ito leaves his sandals outside of the house. I leave my shoes outside also. Looking down at them I think, *Once I wore no shoes.*

From this time on, when inside someone's home, I go in stocking feet.

"Why do you remove your shoes, hermanito?" Toño asks.

"For respect to the floor," I say. And to myself, I think, *And to remind me of home, where I was shoeless.*

This small place of Mr. James Ito has not one speck of dust anywhere. It is without many furnitures and neat neat. In the entry there is nothing but a grainy photograph, just one, black–and–white, hanging like a holy thing. It shows a field stretching away away, and in the furrows a family pausing from their work, grinning, all happily. One of these people, I believe, is Mr. James Ito, but young young.

The picture at once gives me a pang for home. For our milpita. I go close to it. "What grows there?" I ask, hoping for corn.

"Strawberries," Mr. James Ito says. His voice is quiet, his eyes sad.

Quickly I look away and notice a surprising thing that I cannot stop staring at. I walk up to it and smile, for this is the tiniest tree that I have ever seen. Also the most beautiful, with its perfect little leaves, its graceful little branches. And the tiny plot of earth that holds it seems to say, *I am the land, a small piece but precious.* I am enchanted.

"Do you like this tree?" Mr. James Ito asks me, though his voice says he already knows the answer. The field picture that saddened him he forgets it seems.

"Oh, yes."

"It is a bonsai," he tells me. "A dwarf tree. It took many years to make it so."

"*You* made it this way?"

"I did." No pride. Only truth. His speech is as spare as his home.

"How many years?" I ask.

"Seventy years and I still work."

"What took so long?" I blurt, then feel my face flame from my rudeness.

One of Mr. James Ito's smiles skims his face butterfly-like.

"Patience is the way. It takes a lifetime to create beauty. But one must keep working at it. To add beauty to the world—goodness too—these things are of importance."

The Angels is all flashy and big. Big cars. Big buildings. Big signs. But beauty is right here in the smallest thing.

"May I take its picture?" I ask at my politest.

"Of course."

"*Click.*" There it is, Mr. James Ito's bonsai, for always, thanks to Cejas.

Here, in my new—and old—friend's house I feel Papi and Abue holding my hand from afar, showing me the way.

After the visit I float home.

Toño is already gone but I leave a Post-it where he cannot miss it. It says one word: bonsai.

The bonsai has enchanted me, but it is the strawberry field that haunts me.

XXVII

After seeing the beautiful bonsai I want to grow something. To care for it. Not a tiny tree but something of my own home, also beautiful. For a long time I think on this and at last make a decision. I will grow a plant of chiles. Not bonsai chiles, just regular ones.

Near the sky-scratchers of The Angels there is a big Mexican market. One Saturday Toño goes with me to select a plant. The One. There are many chile plants to choose from—too many—all small, which is what I need. I look. I look. I look more. Till I find the perfect one, leaves green green, fruits red like fire.

"This is it!" I at last announce to Toño when he is almost popping from impatience. "This little plant, I call her Hot Stuff," I tell Toño, for I hope her fruits will be truly picantes.

"Great," he grumbles after the long wait.

My mind has by now turned green. In the plant sense. I am spinning plans already—of how best to care for my little beauty. This little Hot Stuff, she must compete with a most heavenly bonsai tree with seventy years of age.

The little chile plant, she grows superbly (word-of-the-day) from the windowsill of our cocina. When the sun beams upon her, the chiles shine like tiny ornaments of Christmas. Each will offer a taste of home.

When we are cooking, we can walk up and take a chile or two from the living plant and toss them into the cook pot to hotten things up. Whenever I take a chile, I always bow a little bow like Mr. James Ito and to the generous little plant I say, "Muchas gracias."

Another Saturday I go again to the market and I buy bean plants. Along with chiles, I will grow frijoles.

"Tell me about the field," I say when I visit Mr. James Ito again. "Please," I add to soften the words. I know I should not be so pushing with my curiosity, but the photograph, I cannot shake it from my heart.

Again Mr. James Ito's eyes go sad. A skin of memory darkens them. For a long time there is silence, then Mr. James Ito says only, "It is gone."

"And the people?"

"Gone."

Not one to give dear details, he leaves it at that.

Heartbreak fills the room. I wait.

"Pearl Harbor came," he tells me in a speech very big for him. "Japanese Americans like me were locked up. Our family field was taken, the field I grew up in. The field of my heart."

Silence again.

"What did you do?"

His eyes go darker. As if he is seeing something that I cannot see.

"I became a soldier. For my country."

My words come slowly. "For Japan?"

"For the United States of America."

We go quiet for a moment. Then I say, "I would never want to kill people." I have seen enough death already.

"Yes," muses Mr. James Ito looking off into somewhere far away. "Killing, in the end, answers nothing."

"You have a gun?" I ask Mr. James Ito, thinking how could this peace man own such a thing.

"I did. But when the war was over and I was going home, I took my rifle apart piece by piece and flung it into the sea."

After this hard talk we both fall silent, and I hope for his words of wisdom to come. Instead, he says something surprising.

"Sometimes," says Mr. James Ito as if in another world, "when I am least expecting it, I catch the scent of strawberries."

A great longing overcomes me. Suddenly I wish to stand among the rich dark furrows with Guapo and Trini, alongside my family, to hear the shuffling plants of maíz, to smell the earth.

I walk home, the milpita filling my soul.

XXVIII

My Abue fills my thoughts.

"Look for signs. Follow them."

I look, but they do not come. "Go your way, Manuelito," Abue says when we talk, "but seeking with your heart. Only then," she says, "will magical things happen."

So I keep trying to do this. I feel always now an unrest. Stronger than before. What is the path for me?

The Angels, it is an okay city, maybe even a great one. But here life is fast fast. Cars. Buses. Motorcycles. And cell phones cell phones cell phones. Everybody is connected, but I believe that nobody is. They just talk, but not to faces. It is all speed and brains numb from phones and advertisings. Toño says that some people count up every step they take. All day. Imagine! Instead of living, they count footsteps! Crazy beyond crazy! I remember what I thought when I first saw this place. That maybe this L.A. is another kind of beast—one that dazes you to death.

Almost any day the sky here is gray. Where are the wild blue sky acres? Where is the beauty? Everything is buildings. Freeways. Streets. Sidewalks of concrete. Where is the land?

The strangest thing. One day, near where we live, I come upon a plant of maíz. By itself. Alone. I am struck with wonder. Why have I never seen this one before? Suddenly I sense a great stillness. Like an angel passing.

This corn is struggling to grow through a crack in the sidewalk. It is stunted. Short. But it is green. In spite of drought, it holds out its arms with hope and waits for rain.

Each day after this, I visit the plant, bringing it water in a little bowl. I stop and stand beside it.

"Hola, Señor Maíz," I say with respect. "I bring you water so that you will grow tall." I hold out my arms like the plant of corn. I realize that we two are the same, struggling to survive in this place of cement where beauty is hiding hiding. Struggling where we cannot truly live, where we do not truly belong.

When I first see it, in my mind I place a circle of magic around the corn. Here, to this plant, is where I come to find my thoughts. Here I sit down inside the circle, a place of safety for me. And I think of what I will do for my life. On what path to place my feet. Passersby do not seem to notice a young man sitting beside a corn plant in the middle of a magic circle, seeking. Of course they do not. This is Los Angeles.

One night I dream of the corn plant. It is no longer growing in a city sidewalk, but instead sprouts up from a field near our pueblito. The plant grows fast—up up up—reaching higher and higher before my eyes. And it begins singing. Words I cannot make out, and yet I know their meaning. Taller taller it grows, to fantastic size, till its wide shadow shelters a small corn plot. Ours.

I wake from the dream and sit upright. *Look for signs. Follow them.* I hear Abue's voice again. Out of the mist of this dream, one thing becomes clear

clear. Dreams change. Once my dream was to be with Toño. No longer. All that has happened has led me to *this* moment. My mother dying, Toño leaving, The Beast journey, Señor Santos, Cejas, Serafina, Mr. James Ito with his field and bonsai. These things have pointed the way my heart has been seeking all along. There have been hints. But the small plant of corn, my deep heart knows, it is my true sign.

For some time I stay in bed without moving, in the absolute and holy stillness.

Long ago my Abue told me that within me I held all of the family dreams. I know now what she meant, that I should stay with them, to tend our little plot. Now—in the quiet, in the dark alone—I know what I will do. I will go home.

No border patrol will stop me from leaving. Probably they will give me a heavy shove to go. I come from People of Corn. I will return to my family and be happy again with the small things of life. I will do what Flores people have always done. Like my father and grandfather and all those before them I will walk behind an ox and plow the dirt and the dust will lift and shawl down upon me like a prayer, the dust, the very breath of the earth. I will tend our milpita and the maíz that it gives. I will be a tiller, a planter, a keeper of the land. Beneath both sun and rain, with my sons and daughters, and their sons and daughters I will labor. Sí, I Manuel Flores will become a farmer.

The absence-pain, it is hurting my heart already. To say goodbye to Mr. James Ito, that will be hard. But in his sage way he will understand. He has lost the field of his heart. He will want me to return to mine.

To break away from Toño is a different thing. How do you tell your brother that you are leaving, that you know you will never see him again? I begin to plan words in my mind. *Do not miss me. Do not be sad. No matter how far away, I am here always by your side.* Using Abue's words I will say, *Hold on to my hand even when I have gone away from you.*

As I plan, a deep ache grows. Toño. It was a terrible struggle to reach him. It will be a harder struggle to let him go. How will I do this without breaking both of our hearts? Impossible. But how can I break them softly?

My words seem rough. Not good enough. I keep thinking, but I cannot make them come out right. I cannot sleep. Then, once as dawn approaches and the sun begins to turn the gray sky gold, I realize something. I need no words.

That afternoon, when Toño wakes up, I am waiting for him in the kitchen. From sleepy eyes he looks at me and I look back, long long. I stand up. I embrace my brother. And he knows.

*Q*uiet beyond quiet. Only the grillos are singing. The dust of the land scents the night.
Above him, the wide sweep of sky is span-
gled with stars. But the young man does not know
this. His eyes are only upon the adobe house, ahead
a small distance.

An old dog of once great ferocity awakens. In
his throat a growl begins. Then by some deep spell
the growl becomes a whine. Suddenly, the dog
stands beside the one who is coming.

And he dances in the dust like a thing possessed.
And he licks the hand of the limping young man.
The young man ruffles the big bucket head, holds
the old dog close to his breast. He kneels to touch the
blessed earth and then—he is rushing rushing, for
the house.

GLOSSARY

a machetazos—By machete blows.

abrazo—Embrace, hug.

Abue—Short for abuelita, grandmother.

¡Alto!—Stop!

asesinos—Killers.

aterrado—Terrified.

azúcar—Sugar.

Bandidos—Bandits.

Belén—A girl's name.

Bestia—Beast.

brincar—To jump.

bruja—Witch.

cabrón—Jerk.

cacahuates—Peanuts.

café—Coffee.

cálmate—Calm down.

casa—House.

Cejas—Eyebrows.

chile—Chili pepper.

chones—Slang for calzones, underwear.

cocina—Kitchen.

comales—Griddles.

compañero—Comrade.

completamente—Completely.

coyote—Paid smuggler of migrants across borders.

desayuno—Breakfast.

diez—Ten.

dinero—Money.

¡Dios mío!—My God!

dulces—Sweets.

el—The (masculine).

El Alacrán—The Scorpion.

El Chavo Viejo—The Old Kid.

El Norte—The North, United States.

eucalipto—Eucalyptus tree.

exceso—Excess.

fantasmas—Phantoms.

frijoles—Beans.

frontera—Border.

Gansitos—Little Geese (brand name).

gracias—Thank you.

gracias a Dios—Thank God.

grillos—Crickets.

Gringolandia—United States.

guarros—Pigs.

hasta—Until.

hermanito—Little brother.

hermano—Brother.

hola—Hello.

¡*Idiota!*—Idiot!

¡*Igual!*—Same to you!

inquieto—Restless.

la—The (feminine).

¡*Ladrona!*—Thief!

"*Las mañanitas*"—Mexican birthday song.

lobo—Wolf.

loco—Crazy.

Los Intensos—The intense ones.

maíz—Corn.

maldito—Bad guy.

'mano—Bro.

¡Me mataron!—They killed me!

"México lindo y querido"—Mexico lovely and dear (song title).

mi viejito—My old man.

milpita—Little corn plot.

momia—Mummy.

monstruo—Monster.

morral—Bag.

muchas gracias—Many thanks.

¡Muévete, güey!—Move it, moron!

niño—Child.

no problema—Spanglish for no problem.

nopales—Prickly pear cactus.

novia—Girlfriend.

órale—Hurry up.

oye, chavo—Listen, kid.

palomitas—Popcorn.

panza—Belly.

papas—Potatoes.

Pásale—Come in.

pelo—Hair.

pelón—Bald.

pena—Embarrassment.

¡Pendejo!—Moron, dummy.

pesitos—Little pesos.

peso—Mexican money.

petate—Woven mat.

picantes—Spicy.

Pingüinos—Penguins (brand name).

poco a poco—Little by little.

polis—Police.

pollito—Chick.

popó—Dung.

por Dios—For God's sake.

pueblito—Small village.

¡Púfalas!—Poof!

pulgada—Inch.

pulpo—Octopus.

Que Dios lo bendiga a usted—God bless you (formal).

Que Dios te bendiga—God bless you (informal).

qué guapo—How handsome.

¡Qué lástima!—What a pity!

¡Qué rico!—How delicious!

ramo—Bouquet.

rateros—Thieves.

relámpago—Lightning.

Río Bravo—A river that is a natural border between parts of Mexico and the United States (where it is called the Rio Grande).

ruedacacas—Dung beetles.

sarape—Shawl.

Señor—Mister.

Señora—Lady.

sí—Yes.

simpático—Likeable.

¡Socorro!—Help!

solamente sal—Only salt.

¡Suerte!—Good luck!

tamal—Tamale, cornmeal mixture with filling like pork.

Tejas—Texas.

tejas—Tiles.

tiendita—Small store.

tipos—Guys.

tlayudas—Large, chewy tortillas.

tortas—Sandwiches.

trabalenguas—Tongue twister.

tren—Train.

un—One (masculine).

vaqueros—Cowboy movies.

Vaya con Dios—Go with God.

Váyase, señora—Go, lady.

velas—Candles.

viajando de mosca—Traveling like a fly.

Vida—Life.

vocabulario—Vocabulary.

AUTHORS' NOTE

L a Bestia, The Beast, is a network of freight trains that move from southern Mexico to the U.S. border. The routes spiderweb out in many directions. Each year thousands of people from Central America and Mexico, fleeing gangs, drug dealers, poverty, or all of these, leave their families and ride the rails seeking refuge and jobs in the United States, which they call the Promised Land. Some desperate riders take their young children along. Sometimes children go alone. Some, like Manuel of this story, are searching for family members who left them behind for similar reasons.

La Bestia is a deadly way to travel. Getting on and staying on are hard in themselves. Sometimes a rider goes to sleep and falls from the train, to be maimed or killed. Sometimes people fall from the lurching motion alone—or are pushed off. Gangs swarm the tops of train cars looking for victims to rob. Assaults on girls and women are common. Along the way are checkpoints patrolled by Mexican immigration authorities. Thugs working with police roam train stops where riders jump off to find food, water or to change trains. Forced to be forever vigilant, riders suffer from constant exhaustion.

Not everybody is a villain. Most travelers on this cruel trip help one another, sharing food and keeping watch for danger. One town in the state of Veracruz is known for its goodness. When a train slows down there, locals toss food, clothing, water, diapers, sweaters to the Beast Riders.

We, the authors, know places like this, for over the forty-eight years we have been friends, we have traveled with our families extensively, from large towns to remote villages.

Border problems have gone on for some time, but this book began to take shape as we realized the plight of Latinos fleeing to The North was worsening. We read about it in newspapers and books, but also heard accounts through designated third parties because the Beast Riders were too terrified to speak with us directly for fear of being sent back to their countries. We heard about children far from their families, forever scarred by travels that never should have had to be taken.

The actual train routes do not pass exactly where Manuel lives. We have changed them to include a part of Oaxaca that we know well and love. For in the end this is a work of fiction, of imagination, tracing the journey across the tender landscape of a boy's heart.

TJ
MER

ACKNOWLEDGMENTS

Many people generously offered their skills and time in the creation of *Beast Rider*. We would like to thank Ashley Johnston, Bernice Yeung, Carmen Rodriguez, Armida Garaygordobil, and Armando Colina of Galería Arvil, S.A., who have improved the story in all stages. Throughout the process, Ashley facilitated the exchange of documents between writers and publisher. Thanks, too, to Duncan Tonatiuh, author of *Pancho Rabbit and the Coyote,* for sharing his deep knowledge of The Beast. Our gratitude goes to Ingeniero Francisco Gorostiza Perez of Ferrocarriles Nacionales de México (the Mexican national railroad) for his expert input on the history of The Beast, route changes, and other details about Mexican railroad operations. To James P. Folsom, Director of the Gardens, the Huntington, San Marino, California, for sharing his formidable knowledge about plants, particularly those of the region of Oaxaca where the story begins. To Danielle Rudeen, assistant to James Folsom, a gracious and tireless link between us and our information sources in Oaxaca. To S. Gomez for having the courage to relate firsthand experiences at the U.S. border. To Yolanda Castrellón for her efforts in connecting us with those who assist Beast Riders. To Lorenzo Perez for his excellent translations. To María Fierro O'Campo and Tey O'Campo of Kidsland, Berkeley, California, magnificent teachers, who supplied us with the memorable "Lesson of the Octopus." To agent Susan Cohen of Writers House, Inc., for keeping our spirits up when things got tough. And to her capable assistant, Nora Long. To editor Howard Reeves, at Abrams, for his careful readings and insightful questions, always offered with a light touch. To Emily Daluga, Howard's assistant, who kept us on schedule in her graceful way.

To Edel Rodriguez and Hana Anouk Nakamura for creating the stunning jacket and internal graphics. To Marie Oishi for her eagle eye to detail. To Diane Aronson for her careful copyediting. To Tamara Arellano for her painstaking proofreading. To Ana Paula Margain de Rhoads, founder and head of REEDUCA, an NGO dedicated to environmental education projects with schools. Her stories from personal experience as a volunteer at shelters for Beast Riders have been of great value.

Three contributors to the Beast Rider project cannot be thanked enough. The Lunch Bunch, the band of writers to which Tony Johnston belongs includes: Eve Bunting, Jennifer Johnston, Lael Littke, Jane Olson, Luisa Perkins, Susan Goldman Rubin, and Martha Tolles. Without the guidance, dedication, and expert critiquing of this group throughout the writing process, the final result would have been weakened. Jennifer Johnston, architect and engineer, born and raised in Mexico, used her sharp organizational skills, her relentless demand for accuracy, and her natural writing ability to keep us on track. And Dr. Alejandro de Ávila Blomberg, Advisor and Curator of the Textile Museum of Oaxaca and originator and Director of the Botanical Gardens of Oaxaca, gave generously of his remarkable energy and spirit and of his awe-inspiring knowledge in countless areas. His scholarly input on all levels greatly enhanced this story.

ABOUT THE AUTHORS

TONY JOHNSTON has written over one hundred books for children. For ten years she was a master student of renowned children's poet Myra Cohn Livingston. Three of Tony's twenty-three books about Mexico and Latin America are volumes of poetry. She lived in Mexico for fifteen years, where she and her family went on countless outings, collecting handwoven sashes and learning about the country. This collection is now housed in the Textile Museum of Oaxaca. Her children were born and raised in Mexico. They return when they can. Mexico is their second home.

MARÍA ELENA FONTANOT DE RHOADS,
PhD, is a psychotherapist specializing in both individual and family issues and a simultaneous translator of Spanish, English, and French. She is also trained in social work. Her understanding of loss—of family and self—to a person forced to leave his home, to struggle against fearful odds, and to become "someone else" in a new place in order to survive has been a key in creating the character of Manuel. She has offered details of Mexican life, especially in Oaxaca. But most valuable is her insight into the psychological trauma produced by the Beast experience.

TONY AND MARÍA ELENA have combined their knowledge and skills to create a story about the ordeal of one fictional boy to draw attention to the plight of all real Beast Riders.